CHRONICLES ABROAD

Venice

CHRONICLES ABROAD

Venice

Edited by John and Kirsten Miller

CHRONICLE BOOKS
SAN FRANCISCO

Special thanks to Annie Barrows

Printed in Hong Kong.

Library of Congress Cataloging-in-Publication Data
Venice / edited by John and Kirsten Miller.
p. cm. — (Chronicles Abroad)
ISBN 0-8118-0471-2
1. Venice (Italy)—Literary collections. 2. Literature, Modern—
Translations into English. I. Miller, John 1959-
II. Miller, Kirsten 1962- . III. Series.
PN6071.V4V3 1994
808.8'9324531—dc20   93-13594
                          CIP

Editing and design: Big Fish Books
Composition: Jennifer Petersen, Big Fish Books

Distributed in Canada by Raincoast Books,
112 East Third Avenue, Vancouver, B.C. V5T 1C8

10 9 8 7 6 5 4 3 2 1

Chronicle Books
275 Fifth Street
San Francisco, CA 94103

Contents

Henry James

PREFACE

I HAD ROOMS on Riva Schiavoni, at the top of a
house near the passage leading off to San Zaccaria; the
waterside life, the wondrous lagoon spread before me, and
the ceaseless human chatter of Venice came in at my windows, to which I seem to myself to have been constantly
driven, in the fruitless fidget of composition, as if to see
whether, out in the blue channel, the ship of some right
suggestion, of some better phrase, of the next happy twist

---

*American novelist, short-story writer and critic Henry James is known
for his lengthy portraits of gawky Americans and sophisticated, decadent
Europeans. This excerpt is from his 1880 preface to his best-known
work,* Portrait of a Lady.

of my subject, the next true touch for my canvas, mightn't come into sight. But I recall vividly enough that the response most elicited, in general, to these restless appeals was the rather grim admonition that romantic and historic sites, such as the land of Italy abounds in, offer the artist a questionable aid to concentration when they themselves are not to be the subject of it. They are too rich in their own life and too charged with their own meanings merely to help him out with a lame phrase; they draw him away from his small question to their own greater ones; so that, after a little, he feels, while thus yearning toward them in his difficulty, as if he were asking an army of glorious veterans to help him arrest a peddler who has given him the wrong change.

Thomas Mann

DEATH IN VENICE

HE SAW IT once more, that landing-place that takes the breath away, that amazing group of incredible structures the Republic set up to meet the awe-struck eye of the approaching seafarer: the airy splendour of the palace and Bridge of Sighs, the columns of lion and saint on the shore, the glory of the projecting flank of the fairy temple, the vista of gateway and clock. Looking, he thought

---

Artsy, nervous characters dominate all of Thomas Mann's masterpieces, including Buddenbrooks, The Magic Mountain, *and* Tonio Kroger. *His 1912 novella* Death in Venice *is a dark, gripping portrait of artistic decadence and sexual ambiguity.*

that to come to Venice by the station is like entering a palace by the back door. No one should approach, save by the high seas as he was doing now, this most improbable of cities.

The engines stopped. Gondolas pressed alongside, the landing-stairs were let down, customs officials came on board and did their office, people began to go ashore. Aschenbach ordered a gondola. He meant to take up his abode by the sea and needed to be conveyed with his luggage to the landing-stage of the little steamers that ply between the city and the Lido. They called down his order to the surface of the water where the gondoliers were quarreling in dialect. Then came another delay while his trunk was worried down the ladder-like stairs. Thus he was forced to endure the importunities of the ghastly young-old man, whose drunken state obscurely urged him to pay the stranger the honour of a formal farewell. "We wish you a very pleasant sojourn," he babbled, bowing and scraping. "Pray keep us in mind. *Au revoir, excusez et bon jour, votre Excellence."* He drooled, he blinked, he licked the corner of his mouth, the little imperial bristled on his elderly chin. He put the tips of two fingers to his mouth and said thickly: "Give her our love, will you, the p-pretty little dear"—here his upper plate came away and fell down on the lower one. . . . Aschenbach escaped. "Little sweety-sweety-sweetheart" he heard behind him, gurgled and stuttered, as he climbed down the rope stair into the boat.

Is there anyone but must repress a secret thrill, on arriving in Venice for the first time—or returning thither after long absence—and stepping into a Venetian gondola? That singular conveyance, come down unchanged from ballad times, black as nothing else on earth except a coffin—what pictures it calls up of lawless, silent adventures in the plashing night; or even more, what visions of death itself, the bier and solemn rites and last soundless voyage! And has anyone remarked that the seat in such a bark, the arm-chair lacquered in coffin-black and dully black-upholstered, is the softest, most luxurious, most relaxing seat in the world? Aschenbach realized it when he had let himself down at the gondolier's feet, opposite his luggage, which lay neatly composed on the vessel's beak. The rowers still gestured fiercely; he heard their harsh, incoherent tones. But the strange stillness of the water-city seemed to take up their voices gently, to disembody and scatter them over the sea. It was warm here in the harbour. The lukewarm air of the sirocco breathed upon him, he leaned back among his cushions and gave himself to the yielding element, closing his eyes for very pleasure in an indolence as unaccustomed as sweet. "The trip will be short," he thought, and wished it might last forever. They gently swayed away from the boat with its bustle and clamour of voices.

It grew still and stiller all about. No sound but the splash of the oars, the hollow slap of the wave against the steep, black, halbert-shaped beak of the vessel, and one sound more—a muttering by fits and starts, expressed

as it were by the motion of his arms, from the lips of the
gondolier. He was talking to himself, between his teeth.
Aschenbach glanced up and saw with surprise that the
lagoon was widening, his vessel was headed for the open
sea. Evidently it would not do to give himself up to sweet
far niente; he must see his wishes carried out.

"You are to take me to the steamboat landing,
you know," he said, half turning round towards it. The
muttering stopped. There was no reply.

"Take me to the steamboat landing," he repeated,
and this time turned quite round and looked up into the
face of the gondolier as he stood there on his little elevated
deck, high against the pale grey sky. The man had an
unpleasing, even brutish face, and wore blue clothes like a
sailor's, with a yellow sash; a shapeless straw hat with the
braid torn at the brim perched rakishly on his head. His
facial structure, as well as the curling blond moustache
under the short snub nose, showed him to be of non-
Italian stock. Physically rather undersized, so that one

would not have expected him to be very muscular, he pulled vigorously at the oar, putting all his body-weight behind each stroke. Now and then the effort he made curled back his lips and bared his white teeth to the gums. He spoke in a decided, almost curt voice, looking out to sea over his fare's head: "The signore is going to the Lido."

Aschenbach answered: "Yes, I am. But I only took the gondola to cross over to San Marco. I am using the *vaporetto* from there."

"But the signore cannot use the *vaporetto*."

"And why not?"

"Because the *vaporetto* does not take luggage."

It was true. Aschenbach remembered it. He made no answer. But the man's gruff, overbearing manner, so unlike the usual courtesy of his countrymen towards the stranger, was intolerable. Aschenbach spoke again: "That is my own affair. I may want to give my luggage in deposit. You will turn around."

No answer. The oar splashed, the wave struck dull against the prow. And the muttering began anew, the gondolier talked to himself, between his teeth.

What should the traveller do? Alone on the water with this tongue-tied, obstinate, uncanny man, he saw no way of enforcing his will. And if only he did not excite himself, how pleasantly he might rest! Had he not wished the voyage might last forever? The wisest thing—and how much the pleasantest!—was to let matters take their own course. A spell of indolence was upon him; it came from the chair he sat in—this low, black-upholstered arm-chair, so gently rocked at the hands of the despotic boatman in his rear. The thought passed dreamily through Aschenbach's brain that perhaps he had fallen into the clutches of a criminal; it had not power to rouse him to action. More annoying was the simpler explanation: that the man was only trying to extort money. A sense of duty, a recollection, as it were, that this ought to be prevented, made him collect himself to say:

"How much do you ask for the trip?"

And the gondolier, going out over his head, replied: "The signore will pay."

There was an established reply to this; Aschenbach made it, mechanically:

"I will pay nothing whatever if you do not take me where I want to go."

"The signore wants to go to the Lido."

"But not with you."

"I am a good rower, signore. I will row you well."

"So much is true," thought Aschenbach, and again he relaxed. "That is true, you row me well. Even if you mean to rob me, even if you hit me in the back with your oar and send me down to the kingdom of Hades, even then you will have rowed me well."

But nothing of the sort happened. Instead, they fell in with company: a boat came alongside and waylaid them, full of men and women singing to guitar and mandolin. They rowed persistently bow for bow with the gondola and filled the silence that had rested on the waters with their lyric love of gain. Aschenbach tossed money into the hat they held out. The music stopped at once, they rowed away. And once more the gondolier's mutter became audible as he talked to himself in fits and snatches.

Thus they rowed on, rocked by the wash of a steamer returning citywards. At the landing two municipal officials were walking up and down with their hands behind their backs and their faces turned towards the lagoon. Aschenbach was helped on shore by the old man with a boat-hook who is the permanent feature of every landing-stage in Venice; and having no small change to pay the boatman, crossed over into the hotel opposite. His wants were supplied in the lobby; but when he came back his possessions were already on a hand-car on the quay, and gondola and gondolier were gone.

"He ran away, signore," said the old boatman. "A bad lot, a man without a license. He is the only gondolier without one. The others telephoned over, and he knew we were on the look-out, so he made off."

Aschenbach shrugged.

"The signore has had a ride for nothing," said the old man and held out his hat. Aschenbach dropped some coins.

Jeanette Winterson

THE QUEEN OF SPADES

THERE IS A city surrounded by water with watery alleys that do for streets and roads and silted up back ways that only the rats can cross. Miss your way, which is easy to do, and you may find yourself staring at a hundred eyes guarding a filthy place of sacks and bones. Find your way, which is easy to do, and you may meet an old woman in a doorway. She will tell your fortune, depending on your face.

Jeanette Winterson was born into a family of strict Pentecostals in Lancashire in 1959. When her parentally imposed missionary career didn't work out, she started studying English at Oxford. There Winterson wrote her first novel, Oranges Are Not the Only Fruit. *This excerpt is from her recent, very Venetian novel,* The Passion.

This is the city of mazes. You may set off from the same place to the same place every day and never go by the same route. If you do so, it will be by mistake. Your bloodhound nose will not serve you here. Your course in compass reading will fail you. Your confident instructions to passers-by will send them to squares they have never heard of, over canals not listed in the notes.

Although wherever you are going is always in front of you, there is no such thing as straight ahead. No as the crow flies short cut will help you to reach the café just over the water. The short cuts are where the cats go, through the impossible gaps, round corners that seem to take you the opposite way. But here, in this mercurial city, it is required you do awake your faith.

With faith, all things are possible.

Rumour has it that the inhabitants of this city walk on water. That, more bizarre still, their feet are webbed. Not all feet, but the feet of the boatmen whose trade is hereditary.

This is the legend.

When a boatman's wife finds herself pregnant she waits until the moon is full and the night empty of idlers. Then she takes her husband's boat and rows to a terrible island where the dead are buried. She leaves her boat with rosemary in the bows so that the limbless ones cannot return with her and hurries to the grave of the most recently dead in her family. She has brought her offerings: a flask of wine, a lock of hair from her husband and a silver coin. She must leave the offerings on the grave and beg for a clean heart if her child be a girl and boatman's feet if her child be a boy. There is no time to lose. She must be home before dawn and the boat must be left for a day and a night covered in salt. In this way, the boatmen keep their secrets and their trade. No newcomer can compete. And no boatman will take off his boots, no matter how you bribe him. I have seen tourists throw diamonds to the fish, but I have never seen a boatman take off his boots.

There was once a weak and foolish man whose

wife cleaned the boat and sold the fish and brought up their children and went to the terrible island as she should when her yearly time was due. Their house was hot in summer and cold in winter and there was too little food and too many mouths. This boatman, ferrying a tourist from one church to another, happened to fall into conversation with the man and the man brought up the question of the webbed feet. At the same time he drew a purse of gold from his pocket and let it lie quietly in the bottom of the boat. Winter was approaching, the boatman was thin and he thought what harm could it do to unlace just one boot and let this visitor see what there was. The next morning, the boat was picked up by a couple of priests on their way to Mass. The tourist was babbling incoherently and pulling at his toes with his fingers. There was no boatman. They took the tourist to the madhouse, San Servelo, a quiet place that caters for the well-off and defective. For all I know, he's still there.

And the boatman?

He was my father.

I never knew him because I wasn't born when he disappeared.

A few weeks after my mother had been left with an empty boat she discovered she was pregnant. Although her future was uncertain and she wasn't strictly speaking married to a boatman any more, she decided to go ahead with the gloomy ritual, and on the appropriate night she rowed her way silently across the lagoon. As she fastened the boat, an owl flew very low and caught her on the shoulder with its wing. She was not hurt but she cried out and stepped back and, as she did so, dropped the sprig of rosemary into the sea. For a moment she thought of returning straight away but, crossing herself, she hurried to her father's grave and placed her offerings. She knew her husband should have been the one, but he had no grave. How like him, she thought, to be as absent in death as he was in life. Her deed done, she pushed off from the shore that even the crabs avoided and later covered the boat in so much salt that it sank.

The Blessed Virgin must have protected her. Even before I was born she had married again. This time, a prosperous baker who could afford to take Sundays off.

The hour of my birth coincided with an eclipse of the sun and my mother did her best to slow down her labour until it had passed. But I was as impatient then as I am now and I forced my head out while the midwife was downstairs heating some milk. A fine head with a crop of red hair and a pair of eyes that made up for the sun's eclipse.

A girl.

It was an easy birth and the midwife held me upside down by the ankles until I bawled. But it was when they spread me out to dry that my mother fainted and the midwife felt forced to open another bottle of wine.

My feet were webbed.

There never was a girl whose feet were webbed in the entire history of the boatmen. My mother in her swoon had visions of rosemary and blamed herself for her carelessness. Or perhaps it was her carefree pleasure with the baker she should blame herself for? She hadn't thought of my father since his boat had sunk. She hadn't thought of him much while it was afloat. The midwife took out her knife with the thick blade and proposed to cut off the offending parts straight away. My mother weakly nodded, imagining I would feel no pain or that pain for a moment would be better than embarrassment for a lifetime. The midwife tried to make an incision in the translucent triangle between my first two toes but her knife sprang from the skin leaving no mark. She tried again and again in between all the toes on each foot. She bent the point of the knife, but that was all.

"It's the Virgin's will," she said at last, finishing the bottle. "There's no knife can get through that."

My mother started to weep and wail and continued in this way until my stepfather came home. He was a man of the world and not easily put off by a pair of webbed feet.

"No one will see so long as she wears shoes and when it comes to a husband, why it won't be the feet he'll be interested in."

This comforted my mother somewhat and we passed the next eighteen years in a normal family way.

Since Bonaparte captured our city of mazes in 1797, we've more or less abandoned ourselves to pleasure. What else is there to do when you've lived a proud and free life and suddenly you're not proud and free any more? We became an enchanted island for the mad, the rich, the bored, the perverted. Our glory days were behind us but our excess was just beginning. That man demolished our churches on a whim and looted our treasures. That woman of his has jewels in her crown that come out of St. Mark's. But of all sorrows, he has our living horses cast by men who stretched their arms between the Devil and God and imprisoned life in a brazen form. He took them from the Basilica and has thrown them up in some readymade square in that tart of towns, Paris.

There were four churches that I loved, which stood looking out across the lagoon to the quiet islands that lie about us. He tore them down to make a public garden. Why did we want a public garden? And if we had and if we had chosen it ourselves we would never have filled it with hundreds of pines laid out in regimental rows. They say Joséphine's a botanist. Couldn't she have found us something a little more exotic? I don't hate the French. My father likes them. They've made his business thrive with their craving for foolish cakes.

He gave me a French name too.

Villanelle. It's pretty enough.

I don't hate the French. I ignore them.

When I was eighteen I started to work the Casino. There aren't many jobs for a girl. I didn't want to go into the bakery and grow old with red hands and forearms like thighs. I couldn't be a dancer, for obvious reasons, and what I would have most liked to have done, worked the boats, was closed to me on account of my sex.

I did take a boat out sometimes, rowing alone for hours up and down the canals and out into the lagoon. I learned the secret ways of boatmen, by watching and by instinct.

If ever I saw a stern disappearing down a black, inhospitable-looking waterway, I followed it and discovered the city within the city that is the knowledge of a few. In this inner city are thieves and Jews and children with slant eyes who come from the eastern wastelands without father or mother. They roam in packs like the cats and the rats and they go after the same food. No one knows why they are here or on what sinister vessel they arrived. They seem to die at twelve or thirteen and yet they are always replaced. I've watched them take a knife to each other for a filthy pile of chicken.

There are exiles too. Men and women driven out of their gleaming palaces that open so elegantly on to shining canals. Men and women who are officially dead according to the registers of Paris. They're here, with the odd bit of gold plate stuffed in a bag as they fled. So long as the Jews will buy the plate and the plate holds out, they survive. When you see the floating corpses belly upwards, you know the gold is ended.

One woman who kept a fleet of boats and a string of cats and dealt in spices lives here now, in the silent city. I cannot tell how old she may be, her hair is green with slime from the walls of the nook she lives in. She feeds on vegetable matter that snags against the stones when the tide is sluggish. She has no teeth. She has no need for teeth. She still wears the curtains that she dragged from her drawing-room window as she left. One curtain she wraps round herself and the other she drapes over her shoulders like a cloak. She sleeps like this.

I've spoken to her. When she hears a boat go by her head pokes out of her nook and she asks you what time of day it might be. Never what time it is; she's too much of a philosopher for that. I saw her once, at evening, her ghoulish hair lit by a lamp she has. She was spreading pieces of rancid meat on a cloth. There were wine goblets beside her.

"I'm having guests to dinner," she shouted, as I glided past on the other side. "I would have invited you, but I don't know your name."

"Villanelle," I shouted back.

"You're a Venetian, but you wear your name as a disguise. Beware the dice and games of chance."

She turned back to her cloth and, although we met again, she never used my name, nor gave any sign that she recognized me.

I WENT TO work in the Casino, raking dice and spreading cards and lifting wallets where I could. There was a cellarful of champagne drunk every night and a cruel dog kept hungry to deal with anyone who couldn't pay. I dressed as a boy because that's what the visitors liked to see. It was part of the game, trying to decide which sex was hidden behind tight breeches and extravagant face-paste . . .

IT WAS AUGUST. Bonaparte's birthday and a hot night. We were due for a celebration ball in the Piazza San Marco, though what we Venetians had to celebrate was not clear. In keeping with our customs, the ball was to be fancy dress and the Casino was arranging outdoor gaming tables and booths of chance. Our city swarmed with French and Austrian pleasure-seekers, the usual bewildered stream of English and even a party of Russians intent on finding satisfaction. Satisfying our guests is what we do best. The price is high but the pleasure is exact.

I made up my lips with vermilion and overlaid my face with white powder. I had no need to add a beauty spot, having one of my own in just the right place. I wore my yellow Casino breeches with the stripe down each side of the leg and a pirate's shirt that concealed my breasts. This was required, but the moustache I added was for my own amusement. And perhaps for my own protection. There are too many dark alleys and too many drunken hands on festival nights.

Across our matchless square that Bonaparte had contemptuously called the finest drawing-room in Europe, our engineers had rigged a wooden frame alive with gunpowder. This was to be triggered at midnight and I was optimistic that, with so many heads looking up, so many pockets would be vulnerable.

The ball began at eight o'clock and I began my night drawing cards in the booth of chance.

Queen of spades you win, Ace of clubs you lose. Play again. What will you risk? Your watch? Your house? Your mistress? I like to smell the urgency on them. Even the calmest, the richest, have that smell. It's somewhere between fear and sex. Passion I suppose.

There's a man who comes to play Chance with me most nights at the Casino. A large man with pads of flesh on his palms like baker's dough. When he squeezes my neck from behind, the sweat on his palms makes them squeak. I always carry a handkerchief. He wears a green waistcoat and I've seen him stripped to that waistcoat because he can't let the dice roll without following it. He has funds. He must have. He spends in a moment what I earn in a month. He's cunning though, for all his madness at the table. Most men wear their pockets or their purses on their sleeves when they're drunk. They want everyone to know how rich they are, how fat with gold. Not him. He has a bag down his trousers and he dips into it with his back turned. I'll never pick that one.

I don't know what else might be down there.

He wonders the same thing about me. I catch him staring at my crotch and now and again I wear a codpiece to taunt him. My breasts are small, so there's no cleavage to give me away, and I'm tall for a girl, especially a Venetian.

I wonder what he'd say to my feet.

Tonight, he's wearing his best suit and his moustache gleams. I fan the cards before him; close them, shuffle them, fan them again. He chooses. Too low to win. Choose again. Too high. Forfeit. He laughs and tosses a coin across the counter.

"You've grown a moustache since two days ago."

"I come from a hairy family."

"It suits you." His eyes stray as usual, but I am firmly behind the booth. He takes out another coin. I spread. The Jack of hearts. An ill-omened card but he doesn't think so, he promises to return and taking the Jack with him for luck moves over to the gaming table. His bottom strains his jacket. They're always taking the cards. I wonder whether to get out another pack or just cheat the next customer. I think that will depend on who the next customer might be.

I LOVE THE night. In Venice, a long time ago, when we had our own calendar and stayed aloof from the world, we began the days at night. What use was the sun to us when our trade and our secrets and our diplomacy depended on darkness? In the dark you are in disguise and this is the city of disguises. In those days (I cannot place them in time because time is to do with daylight), in those days when the sun went down we opened our doors and slid along the eely waters with a hooded light in our prow. All our boats were black then and left no mark on the water where they sat. We were dealing in perfume and silk. Emeralds and diamonds. Affairs of State. We didn't build our bridges simply to avoid walking on water. Nothing so obvious. A bridge is a meeting place. A neutral place. A casual place. Enemies will choose to meet on a bridge and end their quarrel in that void. One will cross to the other side. The other will not return. For lovers, a bridge is a possibility, a metaphor of their chances. And for the traffic in whispered goods, where else but a bridge in the night?

We are a philosophical people, conversant with the nature of greed and desire, holding hands with the

Devil and God. We would not wish to let go of either. This living bridge is tempting to all and you may lose your soul and find it here.

And our own souls?

They are Siamese.

Nowadays, the dark has more light than in the old days. There are flares everywhere and soldiers like to see the streets lit up, like to see some reflection on the canals. They don't trust our soft feet and thin knives. None the less, darkness can be found; in the under-used waterways or out on the lagoon. There's no dark like it. It's soft to the touch and heavy in the hands. You can open your mouth and let it sink into you till it makes a close ball in your belly. You can juggle with it, dodge it, swim in it. You can open it like a door.

The old Venetians had eyes like cats that cut the densest night and took them through impenetrable ways without stumbling. Even now, if you look at us closely you will find that some of us have slit eyes in the daylight.

I used to think that darkness and death were probably the same. That death was the absence of light. That death was nothing more than the shadow-lands where people bought and sold and loved as usual but with less conviction. The night seems more temporary than the day, especially to lovers, and it also seems more uncertain. In this way it sums up our lives, which are uncertain and temporary. We forget about that in the day. In the day we go on for ever. This is the city of uncertainty, where routes and faces look alike and are not. Death will be like that. We will be forever recognizing people we have never met.

But darkness and death are not the same.

The one is temporary, the other is not.

OUR FUNERALS ARE fabulous affairs. We hold them at night, returning to our dark roots. The black boats skim the water and the coffin is crossed with jet. From my upper window that overlooks two intersecting canals, I once saw a rich man's cortège of fifteen boats (the number must be odd) glide out to the lagoon. At the same moment, a pauper's boat, carrying a coffin not varnished but covered in pitch, floated out too, rowed by an old woman with scarcely enough strength to drag the oars. I thought they would collide, but the rich man's boatmen pulled away. Then his widow motioned with her hand and the cortège opened the line at the eleventh boat and made room for the pauper, tossing a rope round the prow so that the old woman had only to guide her craft. They continued thus towards the terrible island of San Michele and I lost sight of them.

For myself, if I am to die, I would like to do it alone, far from the world. I would like to lie on the warm stone in May until my strength is gone, then drop gently into the canal. Such things are still possible in Venice.

NOWADAYS, THE NIGHT is designed for the pleasure-seekers and tonight, by their reckoning, is a *tour de force.* There are fire-eaters frothing at the mouth with yellow tongues. There is a dancing bear. There is a troupe of little girls, their sweet bodies hairless and pink, carrying sugared almonds in copper dishes. There are women of every kind and not all of them are women. In the centre of the square, the workers on Murano have fashioned a huge glass slipper that is constantly filled and re-filled with champagne. To drink from it you must lap like a dog and how these visitors love it. One has already drowned, but what is one death in the midst of so much life?

From the wooden frame above where the gunpowder waits there are also suspended a number of nets and trapezes. From here acrobats swing over the square, casting grotesque shadows on the dancers below. Now and again, one will dangle by the knees and snatch a kiss from whoever is standing below. I like such kisses. They fill the mouth and leave the body free. To kiss well one must kiss solely. No groping hands or stammering hearts. The lips and the lips alone are the pleasure. Passion is sweeter split strand by strand. Divided and re-divided like mercury then gathered up only at the last moment.

You see, I am no stranger to love.

It's getting late, who comes here with a mask over her face? Will she try the cards?

She does. She holds a coin in her palm so that I have to pick it out. Her skin is warm. I spread the cards. She chooses. The ten of diamonds. The three of clubs. Then the Queen of spades.

"A lucky card. The symbol of Venice. You win."

She smiled at me and pulling away her mask revealed a pair of grey-green eyes with flecks of gold. Her cheekbones were high and rouged. Her hair, darker and redder than mine.

"Play again?"

She shook her head and had a waiter bring over a bottle of champagne. Not any champagne. Madame Clicquot. The only good thing to come out of France. She held the glass in a silent toast, perhaps to her own good fortune. The Queen of spades is a serious win and one we are usually careful to avoid. Still she did not speak, but watched me through the crystal and suddenly draining her glass stroked the side of my face. Only for a second she touched me and then she was gone and I was left with my heart smashing at my chest and three-quarters of a bottle of the best champagne. I was careful to conceal both.

I am pragmatic about love and have taken my pleasure with both men and women, but I have never needed a guard for my heart. My heart is a reliable organ.

AT MIDNIGHT THE gunpowder was triggered and the sky above St. Mark's broke into a million coloured pieces. The fireworks lasted perhaps half an hour and during that time I was able to finger enough money to bribe a friend to take over my booth for a while. I slipped through the press towards the still bubbling glass slipper looking for her.

She had vanished. There were faces and dresses and masks and kisses to be had and a hand at every turn but she was not there. I was detained by an infantryman who held up two glass balls and asked if I would exchange them for mine. But I was in no mood for charming games and pushed past him, my eyes begging for a sign.

The roulette table. The gaming table. The fortune tellers. The fabulous three-breasted woman. The singing ape. The double-speed dominoes and the tarot.

She was not there.

She was nowhere.

My time was up and I went back to the booth of chance full of champagne and an empty heart.

"There was a woman looking for you," said my friend. "She left this."

On the table was an earring. Roman by the look of it, curiously shaped, made of that distinct old yellow gold that these times do not know.

I put it in my ear and, spreading the cards in a

perfect fan, took out the Queen of spades. No one else should win tonight. I would keep her card until she needed it.

GAIETY SOON AGES.

By three o'clock the revellers were drifting away through the arches around St. Mark's or lying in piles by the cafés, opening early to provide strong coffee. The gaming was over. The Casino tellers were packing away their gaudy stripes and optimistic baize. I was off-duty and it was almost dawn. Usually, I go straight home and meet my stepfather on his way to the bakery. He slaps me about the shoulder and makes some joke about how much money I'm making. He's a curious man; a shrug of the shoulders and a wink and that's him. He's never thought it odd that his daughter cross-dresses for a living and sells second-hand purses on the side. But then, he's never thought it odd that his daughter was born with webbed feet.

"There are stranger things," he said.

And I suppose there are.

This morning, there's no going home. I'm bolt upright, my legs are restless and the only sensible thing is to borrow a boat and calm myself in the Venetian way; on the water.

THE GRAND CANAL is already busy with vegetable boats. I am the only one who seems intent on recreation and the others eye me curiously, in between steadying a load or arguing with a friend. These are my people, they can eye me as much as they wish.

I push on, under the Rialto, that strange half-bridge that can be drawn up to stop one half of this city warring with the other. They'll seal it eventually and we'll be brothers and mothers. But that will be the doom of paradox.

Bridges join but they also separate.

OUT NOW, PAST the houses that lean into the water. Past the Casino itself. Past the money-lenders and the churches and the buildings of state. Out now into the lagoon with only the wind and the seagulls for company.

There is a certainty that comes with the oars, with the sense of generation after generation standing up like this and rowing like this with rhythm and ease. This city is littered with ghosts seeing to their own. No family would be complete without its ancestors.

Our ancestors. Our belonging. The future is foretold from the past and the future, the present is partial. All time is eternally present and so all time is ours. There is no sense in forgetting and every sense in dreaming. Thus the present is made rich. Thus the present is made whole. On the lagoon this morning, with the past at my elbow, rowing beside me, I see the future glittering on the water. I catch sight of myself in the water and see in the distortions of my face what I might become.

If I find her, how will my future be?

I will find her.

Somewhere between fear and sex passion is.

Passion is not so much an emotion as a destiny. What choice have I in the face of this wind but to put up sail and rest my oars?

Dawn breaks.

I spent the weeks that followed in a hectic stupor.

Is there such a thing? There is. It is the condition that most resembles a particular kind of mental disorder. I have seen ones like me in San Servelo. It manifests itself as a compulsion to be forever doing something, however meaningless. The body must move but the mind is blank.

I walked the streets, rowed circles around Venice, woke up in the middle of the night with covers in impossible knots and my muscles rigid. I took to working double shifts at the Casino, dressing as a woman in the afternoon and a young man in the evenings. I ate when food was put in front of me and slept when my body was throbbing with exhaustion.

I lost weight.

I found myself staring into space, forgetting where I was going.

I was cold.

I never go to confession; God doesn't want us to confess, he want us to challenge him, but for a while I went into our churches because they were built from the heart. Improbable hearts that I had never understood before. Hearts so full of longing that these old stones still cry out with their ecstasy. These are warm churches, built in the sun.

I sat at the back, listening to the music or mumbling through the service. I'm never tempted by God but I like his trappings. Not tempted but I begin to understand why others are. With this feeling inside, with this wild love that threatens, what safe places might there be? Where do you store gunpowder? How do you sleep at night again? If I were a little different I might turn passion into something holy and then I would sleep again. And then my ecstasy would be my ecstasy but I would not be afraid.

My flabby friend, who has decided I'm a woman, has asked me to marry him. He has promised to keep me in luxury and all kinds of fancy goods, provided I go on dressing as a young man in the comfort of our own home. He likes that. He says he'll get my moustaches and codpieces specially made and a rare old time we'll have of it, playing games and getting drunk. I was thinking of pulling a knife on him right there in the middle of the Casino, but my Venetian pragmatism stepped in and I thought I might have a little game myself. Anything now to relieve the ache of never finding her.

I've always wondered where his money comes from. Is it inherited? Does his mother still settle his bills?

No. He earns his money. He earns his money supplying the French army with meat and horses. Meat and horses he tells me that wouldn't normally feed a cat or mount a beggar.

How does he get away with it?

There's no one else who can supply so much so fast, anywhere; as soon as his orders arrive, the supplies are on their way.

It seems that Bonaparte wins his battles quickly or not at all. That's his way. He doesn't need quality, he needs action. He needs his men on their feet for a few days' march and a few days' battle. He needs horses for a single charge. That's enough. What does it matter if the horses are lame and the men are poisoned so long as they last so long as they're needed?

I'D BE MARRYING a meat man.

I LET HIM buy me champagne. Only the best. I hadn't tasted Madame Clicquot since the hot night in August. The rush of it along my tongue and into my throat brought back other memories. Memories of a single touch. How could anything so passing be so pervasive?

But Christ said, "Follow me," and it was done.

SUNK IN THESE dreams, I hardly felt his hand along my leg, his fingers on my belly. Then I was reminded vividly of squid and their suckers and I shook him off shouting that I'd never marry him, not for all the Veuve Clicquot in France nor a Venice full of codpieces. His face was always red so it was hard to tell what he felt about these insults. He got up from where he'd been kneeling and straightened his waistcoat. He asked me if I wanted to keep my job.

"I'll keep my job because I'm good at it and clients like you come through the door every day."

He hit me then. Not hard but I was shocked. I'd never been hit before. I hit him back. Hard.

He started to laugh and coming towards me squashed me flat against the wall. It was like being under a pile of fish. I didn't try to move, he was twice my weight at least and I'm no heroine. I'd nothing to lose either, having lost it already in happier times.

He left a stain on my shirt and threw a coin at

me by way of goodbye.

What did I expect from a meat man?

I went back to the gaming floor.

NOVEMBER IN VENICE is the beginning of the catarrh season. Catarrh is part of our heritage like St. Mark's. Long ago, when the Council of Three ruled in mysterious ways, any traitor or hapless one done away with was usually announced to have died of catarrh. In this way, no one was embarrassed. It's the fog that rolls in from the lagoon and hides one end of the Piazza from another that brings on our hateful congestion. It rains too, mournfully and quietly, and the boatmen sit under sodden rags and stare helplessly into the canals. Such weather drives away the foreigners and that's the only good thing that can be said of it. Even the brilliant water-gate at the Fenice turns grey.

On an afternoon when the Casino didn't want me and I didn't want myself, I went to Florian's to drink and gaze at the Square. It's a fulfilling pastime.

I had been sitting perhaps an hour when I had the feeling of being watched. There was no one near me, but there was someone behind a screen a little way off. I let my mind retreat again. What did it matter? We are always watching or watched. The waiter came over to me with a packet in his hand.

I opened it. It was an earring. It was the pair.

And she stood before me and I realised I was dressed as I had been that night because I was waiting to work. My hand went to my lip.

"You shaved it off," she said.

I smiled. I couldn't speak.

She invited me to dine with her the following evening and I took her address and accepted.

In the Casino that night I tried to decide what to do. She thought I was a young man. I was not. Should I go to see her as myself and joke about the mistake and leave gracefully? My heart shrivelled at this thought. To lose her again so soon. And what was myself? Was this breeches and boots self any less real than my garters? What was it about me that interested her?

You play, you win. You play, you lose. You play.

I was careful to steal enough to buy a bottle of the best champagne.

LOVERS ARE NOT at their best when it matters. Mouths dry up, palms sweat, conversation flags and all the time the heart is threatening to fly from the body once and for all. Lovers have been known to have heart attacks. Lovers drink too much from nervousness and cannot perform. They eat too little and faint during their fervently wished consummation. They do not stroke the favoured cat and their face-paint comes loose. This is not all. Whatever you have set store by, your dress, your dinner, your poetry, will go wrong.

HER HOUSE WAS gracious, standing on a quiet waterway, fashionable but not vulgar. The drawing-room, enormous with great windows at either end and a fireplace that would have suited an idle wolfhound. It was simply furnished; an oval table and a *chaise-longue*. A few Chinese ornaments that she liked to collect when the ships came through. She had also a strange assortment of dead insects mounted in cases on the wall. I had never seen such things before and wondered about this enthusiasm.

She stood close to me as she took me through the house, pointing out certain pictures and books. Her hand guided my elbow at the stairs and when we sat down to eat she did not arrange us formally but put me beside her, the bottle in between.

We talked about the opera and the theatre and the visitors and the weather and ourselves. I told her that my real father had been a boatman and she laughed and asked could it be true that we had webbed feet?

"Of course," I said and she laughed the more at this joke.

We had eaten. The bottle was empty. She said she had married late in life, had not expected to marry at all being stubborn and of independent means. Her husband dealt in rare books and manuscripts from the east. Ancient maps that showed the lairs of griffins and the haunts of whales. Treasure maps that claimed to know the whereabouts of the Holy Grail. He was a quiet and cultured man of whom she was fond.

He was away.

We had eaten, the bottle was empty. There was nothing more that could be said without strain or repetition. I had been with her more than five hours already and it was time to leave. As we stood up and she moved to get something I stretched out my arm, that was all, and she turned back into my arms so that my hands were on her shoulder blades and hers along my spine. We stayed thus for a few moments until I had courage enough to kiss her neck very lightly. She did not pull away. I grew bolder and kissed her mouth, biting a little at the lower lip.

She kissed me.

"I can't make love to you," she said.

Relief and despair.

"But I can kiss you."

And so, from the first, we separated our pleasure. She lay on the rug and I lay at right angles to her so that only our lips might meet. Kissing in this way is the strangest of distractions. The greedy body that clamours for satisfaction is forced to content itself with a single sensation and, just as the blind hear more acutely and the deaf can feel the grass grow, so the mouth becomes the focus of love and all things pass through it and are re-defined. It is a sweet and precise torture.

When I left her house some time later, I did not set off straight away, but watched her moving from room to room extinguishing the lights. Upwards she went, closing the dark behind her until there was only one light left and that was her own. She said she often read into the small hours while her husband was away. Tonight she did not read. She paused briefly at the window and then the house was black.

What was she thinking?

What was she feeling?

I walked slowly through the silent squares and across the Rialto, where the mist was brooding above the water. The boats were covered and empty apart from the cats that make their homes under the seat boards. There was no one, not even the beggars who fold themselves and their rags into any doorway.

HOW IS IT that one day life is orderly and you are content, a little cynical perhaps but on the whole just so, and then without warning you find the solid floor is a trapdoor and you are now in another place whose geography is uncertain and whose customs are strange?

Travellers at least have a choice. Those who set sail know that things will not be the same as at home.

Explorers are prepared. But for us, who travel along the blood vessels, who come to the cities of the interior by chance, there is no preparation. We who were fluent find life is a foreign language. Somewhere between the swamp and the mountains. Somewhere between fear and sex. Somewhere between God and the Devil passion is and the way there is sudden and the way back is worse.

I'm surprised at myself talking in this way. I'm young, the world is before me, there will be others. I feel my first streak of defiance since I met her. My first upsurge of self. I won't see her again. I can go home, throw aside these clothes and move on. I can move out if I like. I'm sure the meat man can be persuaded to take me to Paris for a favour or two.

Passion, I spit on it.

I spat into the canal.

Then the moon came visible between the clouds, a full moon, and I thought of my mother rowing her way in faith to the terrible island.

THE SURFACE OF the canal had the look of polished jet. I took off my boots slowly, pulling the laces loose and easing them free. Enfolded between each toe were my own moons. Pale and opaque. Unused. I had often played with them but I never thought they might be real. My mother wouldn't even tell me if the rumours were real and I have no boating cousins. My brothers are gone away.

Could I walk on that water?

Could I?

I faltered at the slippery steps leading into the dark. It was November, after all. I might die if I fell in. I tried balancing my foot on the surface and it dropped beneath into the cold nothingness.

Could a woman love a woman for more than a night?

I stepped out and in the morning they say a beggar was running round the Rialto talking about a young man who'd walked across the canal like it was solid.

I'm telling you stories. Trust me.

J. W. Goethe

ITALIAN JOURNEYS

September 29, Michaelmas Eve

SO MUCH HAS been said and written about Venice already that I do not want to describe it too minutely. I shall only give my immediate impression. What strikes me most is again the people in their sheer mass and instinctive existence.

Johann Wolfgang Goethe was a German playwright, theatre director, novelist, poet, scientist, and politician. His diverse writings are dotted with provocative titles like Trilogy of Passion, The Metamorphosis of Plants, German Architecture, *and* The Western Divan.
In his spare time, Goethe traveled far and wide; Italian Journeys *is a record of a 1786—88 trip.*

This race did not seek refuge in these islands for fun, nor were those who joined later moved by chance; necessity taught them to find safety in the most unfavourable location. Later, however, this turned out to their greatest advantage and made them wise at a time when the whole northern world still lay in darkness; their increasing population and wealth were a logical consequence. Houses were crowded closer and closer together, sand and swamp transformed into solid pavement. The houses grew upward like closely planted trees and were forced to make up in height for what they were denied in width. Avid for every inch of ground and cramped into a narrow space from the very beginning, they kept the alleys separating two rows of houses narrow, just wide enough to let people pass each other. The place of street and square and promenade was taken by water. In consequence, the Venetian was bound to develop into a new kind of creature, and that is why, too, Venice can only be compared to itself. The Canal Grande, winding snakelike through the town, is unlike any other street in the world, and no square can compete with the vast expanse of water in front of the Piazza San Marco, enclosed on one side by the semicircle of Venice itself. Across it to the left is the island of San Giorgio Maggiore, to the right the Giudecca with its canal, and still further to the right the Dogana with the entrance to the Canal Grande, where stand some great gleaming marble temples. These, in brief, are the chief objects which strike the eye when one leaves the Piazza San Marco between the two columns.

After dinner I hurried out without a guide and, after noting the four points of the compass, plunged into the labyrinth of this city, which is intersected everywhere by canals but joined together by bridges. The compactness of it all is unimaginable unless one has seen it. As a rule, one can measure the width of an alley with one's outstretched arms; in the narrowest, one even scrapes one's elbows if one holds them akimbo; occasionally there is a wider lane and even a little square every so often, but everything is relatively narrow.

I easily found the Canal Grande and its principal bridge, the Ponte Rialto, which is a single arch of white marble. Looking down, I saw the Canal teeming with gondolas and the barges which bring all necessities from the mainland and land at this point to unload. As today is the Feast of St. Michael, the scene was especially full of life.

The Canal Grande, which separates the two main islands of Venice, is only spanned by a single bridge, the Rialto, but it can be crossed in open boats at various points. Today I watched with delight as many well-dressed women in black veils were ferried across on their way to the Church of the Solemnized Archangel. I left the bridge and walked to one of the landing points to get a closer look at them as they left the ferry. There were some beautiful faces and figures among them.

When I felt tired, I left the narrow alleys and

took my seat in a gondola. Wishing to enjoy the view from the opposite side, I passed the northern end of the Canal Grande, round the island of Santa Chiara, into the lagoons, then into the Giudecca Canal and continued as far as the Piazza San Marco. Reclining in my gondola, I suddenly felt myself, as every Venetian does, a Lord of the Adriatic. I thought with piety of my father, for nothing gave him greater pleasure than to talk of these things. It will be the same with me, I know. Everything around me is a worthy, stupendous monument, not to one ruler, but to a whole people. Their lagoons may be gradually silting up and unhealthy miasmas hovering over their marshes, their trade may be declining, their political power dwindling, but this republic will never become a whit less venerable in the eyes of one observer. Venice, like everything else which has a phenomenal existence, is subject to Time.

September 30

TOWARDS EVENING I explored—again without a

guide—the remoter quarters of the city. All the bridges are provided with stairs, so that gondolas and even larger boats can pass under their arches without difficulty. I tried to find my way in and out of the labyrinth by myself, asking nobody the way and taking my directions only from the points of the compass. It is possible to do this and I find my method of personal experience the best. I have been to the furthest edges of the inhabited area and studied the way of life, the morals and manners of the inhabitants. They are different in every district. Good heavens! what a poor good creature man is after all.

Many little houses rise directly from the canals, but here and there are well-paved footpaths on which one can stroll very pleasantly between water, churches and palaces. One agreeable walk is along the stone quay on the northern side. From it one can see the smaller islands, among them Murano, a Venice in miniature. The intervening lagoons are alive with innumerable gondolas.

Evening

TODAY I BOUGHT a map of the city. After studying
it carefully, I climbed the Campanile of San Marco. It was
nearly noon and the sun shone so brightly that I could
recognize both close and distant places without a tele-
scope. The lagoons are covered at high tide, and when I
turned my eyes in the direction of the Lido, a narrow
strip of land which shuts in the lagoons, I saw the sea for
the first time. Some sails were visible on it, and in the
lagoons themselves galleys and frigates were lying at
anchor. These were to have joined Admiral Emo, who is
fighting the Algerians, but unfavourable winds have
detained them here. North and west, the hills of Padua
and Vicenza and the Tirolean Alps made a beautiful
frame to the whole picture.

October 1

TODAY WAS SUNDAY, and as I walked about I was
struck by the uncleanliness of the streets. This set me

thinking. There appears to be some kind of police regulation on this matter, for people sweep the rubbish into corners and I saw large barges stopping at certain points and carrying the rubbish away. They came from the surrounding islands where people are in need of manure. But there is no logic or discipline in these arrangements. The dirt is all the more inexcusable because the city is as designed for cleanliness as any Dutch town. All the streets are paved with flagstones; even in the remotest quarter, bricks are at least placed on the kerb and, wherever it is necessary, the streets are raised in the middle and have gutters at their sides to catch the water and carry it off into covered drains. These and other technical devices are clearly the work of efficient architects who planned to make Venice the cleanest of cities as well as the most unusual. As I walked, I found myself devising sanitary regulations and drawing up a preliminary plan for an imaginary police inspector who was seriously interested in the problem. It shows how eager man always is to sweep his neighbour's doorstep.

October 7

LAST NIGHT, AT the Teatro San Crisostomo, I saw Crébillon's *Electra*—in translation, of course. I cannot express how tasteless I found it and how terribly bored I was.

As a matter of fact, the actors were quite good and knew how to put over certain passages on the public. In one scene alone, Orestes has no less than three separate narrations, all poetically embroidered. Electra, a pretty, vivacious little woman, spoke the verse beautifully, but her acting was as extravagant as her role, alas, demanded. However, I again learned something. The Italian iambic hendecasyllabic is ill-suited to declamation because the last syllable is always short and this causes an involuntary raising of the voice at the end of every line.

This morning I attended High Mass at the Church of Santa Giustina, where, on this day of the year, the Doge has always to be present to commemorate an old victory over the Turks. The gilded barges, carrying the Prince and some of the nobility, land at the little square; oddly liveried boatmen ply their red-painted oars; on shore the clergy and religious orders, holding lighted candles on poles and silver candelabra, jostle each other and stand around waiting; gangways covered with carpets are laid across from the vessels to the shore: first come the *Savii* in their long violet robes, then the Senators in their red ones, and, last, the old Doge, in his long golden gown and ermine cape and wearing his golden Phrygian cap, leaves the barge while three servants bear the train of his robe.

To watch all this happening in a little square before the doors of a church on which Turkish standards were displayed was like seeing an old tapestry of beautiful colour and design, and to me, as a fugitive from the north, it gave keen pleasure. At home, where short coats are de rigueur for all festive occasions and the finest ceremony we can imagine is a parade of shouldered muskets, an affair like this might look out of place, but here these trailing robes and unmilitary ceremonies are perfectly in keeping.

The Doge is a good-looking, imposing man. Although, apparently, in ill health, he holds himself, for the sake of dignity, erect under his heavy gown. He looks like the grandpapa of the whole race and his manner is gracious and courteous. His garments were very becoming and the little transparent bonnet he wore under his cap did not offend the eye, for it rested upon the most lovely snow-white hair.

He was accompanied by about fifty noblemen, most of them very good-looking. I did not see a single ugly one. Some were tall and had big heads, framed in blond curly wigs. As for their faces, the features were prominent and the flesh, though soft and white, had nothing repellently flabby about it. They looked rather intelligent, self-assured, unaffected and cheerful.

When they had all taken their places in the church and High Mass had begun, the religious orders entered in pairs by the west door, were blessed with holy water, bowed to the high altar, to the Doge and to the nobility, and then left by a side door to the right.

FOR THIS EVENING I had made arrangements to hear the famous singing of the boatmen, who chant verses by Tasso and Ariosto to their own melodies. This performance has to be ordered in advance, for it is now rarely done and belongs, rather, to the half-forgotten legends of the past. The moon had risen when I took my seat in a gondola and the two singers, one in the prow, the other in the stern, began chanting verse after verse in turns. The melody, which we know from Rousseau, is something between chorale and recitative. It always moves at the same tempo without any definite beat. The modulation is of the same character; the singers change pitch according to the content of the verse in a kind of declamation.

I shall not go into the question of how the melody evolved. It is enough to say that it is ideal for someone idly singing to himself and adapting the tune to poems he knows by heart.

The singer sits on the shore of an island, on the bank of a canal or in a gondola, and sings at the top of his voice—the people here appreciate volume more than anything else. His aim is to make his voice carry as far as possible over the still mirror of water. Far away another singer hears it. He knows the melody and the words and answers with the next verse. The first singer answers again, and so on. Each is the echo of the other. They keep this up night after night without ever getting tired. If the listener has chosen the right spot, which is halfway between them, the further apart they are, the more enchanting the singing will sound.

To demonstrate this, my boatmen tied up the gondola on the shore of the Giudecca and walked along the canal in opposite directions. I walked back and forth, leaving the one, who was just about to sing, and walking towards the other, who had just stopped.

For the first time I felt the full effect of this singing. The sound of their voices far away was extraordinary, a lament without sadness, and I was moved to tears. I put this down to my mood at the moment, but my old manservant said: *"é singolare, come quel canto intenerisce, e molto più, quando è più ben cantato."* He wanted me to hear the women on the Lido, especially those from Malamocco and Pellestrina. They too, he told me, sing verses by Tasso to the same or a similar melody, and added: "It is their custom to sit on the seashore while their husbands are out sea-fishing, and sing these songs in penetrating tones until, from far out over the sea, their men reply, and in this way they converse with each other." Is this not a beautiful custom? I dare say that, to someone standing close by, the sound of such voices, competing with the thunder of the waves, might not be very agreeable. But the motive behind such singing is so human and genuine that it makes the mere notes of the melody, over which scholars have racked their brains in vain, come to life. It is the cry of some lonely human being sent out into the wide world till it reaches the ears of another lonely human being who is moved to answer it.

October 8

I VISITED THE Palazzo Pisani Moretta to look at a painting by Paolo Veronese. The female members of the family of Darius are kneeling at the feet of Alexander and Hephaestus. The mother mistakes Hephaestus for the King, but he declines the honour and points to the right person. There is a legend connected with this picture according to which Veronese was for a long time an honoured guest in this palace and, to show his gratitude, painted it in secret, rolled it up and left it under his bed as a gift. It is certainly worthy of such an unusual history. His ability to create a harmony through a skillful distribution of light and shade and local colours without any single dominant tone is conspicuous in this painting, which is in a remarkable state of preservation and looks as fresh as if it had been painted yesterday. When a canvas of this kind has suffered any damage, our pleasure in it is spoiled without our knowing the reason.

Once it is understood that Veronese wanted to paint an episode of the sixteenth century, no one is going to criticize him for the costumes. The graded placing of the group, the mother in front, behind her the wife, and then the daughters in order, is natural and happy. The youngest princess, who kneels behind all the rest, is a pretty little mouse with a defiant expression. She looks as if she were not at all pleased at coming last.

My tendency to look at the world through the eyes of the painter whose pictures I have seen last given me an odd idea. Since our eyes are educated from childhood on by the objects we see around us, a Venetian painter is bound to see the world as a brighter and gayer place than most people see it. We northerners who spend our lives in a drab and, because of the dirt and the dust, an uglier country where even reflected light is subdued, and who have, most of us, to live in cramped rooms—we cannot instinctively develop an eye which looks with such delight at the world.

As I glided over the lagoons in the brilliant sunshine and saw the gondoliers in their colourful costume, gracefully posed against the blue sky as they rowed with easy strokes across the light-green surface of the water, I felt I was looking at the latest and best painting of the Venetian school. The sunshine raised the local colours to a dazzling glare and even the parts in shadow were so light that they could have served pretty well as sources of light. The same could be said of the reflections in the water. Everything was painted clearly on a clear background. It only needed the sparkle of a white-crested wave to put the dot on the *i*.

Both Titian and Veronese possessed this clarity to the highest degree, and when we do not find it in their works, this means that the picture has suffered damage or been retouched.

The cupolas, vaults and lateral wall-faces of the Basilica of San Marco are completely covered with mosaics of various colours on a common gold ground. Some are good, some are poor, depending upon the master who made the original cartoon. Everything depends on that, for it is possible to imitate with square little pieces of glass, though not very exactly, either the Good or the Bad.

The art of mosaic, which gave the Ancients their paved floors and the Christians the vaulted Heaven of their churches, has now been degraded to snuff boxes and bracelets. Our times are worse than we think.

Jean Paul Sartre

MY VENETIAN WINDOW

BECAUSE THIS IS not a city, no: it is an archipelago. From your small island you look enviously at the island facing you: over there is . . . what? a solitude, a purity, a silence which is not to be found, you would swear, on this side. Wherever you may be, the true Venice, you will find, is always elsewhere. For me, at least, it is like that.

Jean Paul Sartre, the popularizer of existentialism, meticulously detailed the meaninglessness of life in Nausea *and* Being and Nothingness. *But this philosopher had a soft side: he loved sappy, romantic Venice. This paean to the city is from a 1953 French journal,* Situations IV. *It was translated for the first time by Tony Tanner.*

Usually, I tend rather to content myself with what I have; but in Venice I am the prey of a kind of mad jealousy; if I didn't restrain myself, I would be on bridges and in gondolas the whole time, desperately looking for the secret Venice of the other side. Of course, as soon as I get there, everything fades; I come back: the tranquil mystery has re-formed itself on the other side. There are good times when I simply resign myself: Venice is just exactly the place where I am not. Those princely chalets, opposite me, surely they come up out of the water. Impossible to believe that they float: a house, that doesn't float. Nor do they lie heavily on the lagoon: it would sink under their weight. Nor are they imponderable: you can see quite clearly they are made of bricks, stone and wood. What then? You really have to feel them emerging: you look at the palaces of the Grand Canal from top to bottom and that is enough for you to sense in them a sort of frozen momentum which is, if you like, their density turned upside-down, the inversion of their mass. A splash of petrified water, perhaps: you would say that they had only just appeared and that there had been nothing before these little stubborn erections. In short, they are always slightly apparitional. An apparition—now, you can guess what that would be like: it would take place in an instant and it would make it easier to grasp the following paradox—pure Nothingness would remain and yet Being would already be there. When I look at the Palazzo Dario . . . I always have the feeling that, yes, it is certainly there, but at the same time that there is nothing there. So much so that sometimes it seems as if the whole city had disappeared. One evening, coming back from Murano, my boat found itself alone and out of sight: no more Venice. Somewhere to the left the water rose in clouds under the gold of the sky. Just for a moment all is clear and precise. . . . And then—what is that opposite me? The Other foot-path of a 'residential' avenue, or the Other bank of a river? At any rate, it is the Other. Come to that, the left and the right of the

Canal are hardly distinguishable. To be sure, the
Fondouque des Turcs is on one side, the Ca' d'Oro is on
the other. But, finally, it's always the same caskets, the
same marquetry work, interrupted here and there by the
billowings of large town halls of white marble, gnawed
away by tears of filth. Sometimes, when my gondola has
been gliding between these two funfairs, I have asked
myself which was the reflection of the other. In short, it's
not their differences which distinguish them: on the con-
trary. Imagine that you are approaching a mirror: an
image starts to form there—there is your nose, your eyes,
your mouth, your clothes. It's you, it should be you. And
yet, there is something about the reflection—something
which is neither the green of the eyes, nor the line of the
lips, nor the cut of the clothes; something which makes
you suddenly say—they have put an other in the mirror
in place of my reflection. That is pretty nearly the
impression which the presence of Venice always makes.
Nothing today prevents me from thinking that it's our

funfair which is the real one, and the other only an image, very gently blown eastward by the Adriatic wind.

Lord Byron

CHILDE HAROLD'S PILGRIMAGE

I.

I STOOD IN Venice, on the Bridge of Sighs;
A palace and a prison on each hand:
I saw from out of the wave her structures
    rise
As from the stroke of the enchanter's

Lord Byron was a Scottish poet and creator of the legendary Byronic Hero—the defiant young man who has committed some hidden, abominable sin. Byron's first major work was Childe Harold's Pilgrimage, a fictionalized account of his 1811 Mediterranean journey. The book was a big hit, and the poet went on to a string of successes, culminating in his never-finished masterpiece, Don Juan.

wand:
A thousand years their cloudy wings
    expand
Around me, and a dying Glory smiles
O'er the far times, when many a subject
    land
Look'd to the winged Lion's marble piles,
Where Venice sate in state, throned on her
    hundred isles!

II.

She looks a sea Cybele, fresh from ocean,
Rising with her tiara of proud towers
At airy distance, with majestic motion,
A ruler of the waters and their powers:
And such she was;—her daughters had
    their dowers
From spoils of nations, and the exhaust-
    less East

Pour'd in her lap all gems in sparkling
      showers.
In purple was she robed, and of her feast
Monarchs partook, and deem'd their dignity
      increased.

III.

In Venice Tasso's echoes are no more,
And silent rows the songless gondolier;
Her palaces are crumbling to the shore,
And music meets not always now the
      ear:
Those days are gone—but Beauty still is here.
States fall, arts fade—but Nature doth not
      die,
Nor yet forget how Venice once was dear,
The pleasant place of all festivity,
The revel of the earth, the masque of Italy!

William Murray

THE VENETIAN MASK

VENICE HAS ALWAYS loved a good show. In fact, hardly a week passes now, even during the cold and clammy off-season months from the end of October to late March, without some sort of public celebration in honor of a saint or a notable historical event. Among the grander and best-known examples are the Feast of the Redentore, held on the third Sunday in July to commemorate the end of a plague in 1575 that in two years wiped

William Murray has been the author of The New Yorker's *"Letter from Rome" since 1962. "The Venetian Mask" is from a 1991 collection of his columns,* The Last Italian.

out a third of the population, and the *Regatta Storica*, which dates back to 1300 A.D. and features a highly competitive seven-and-a-half kilometer boat race that awards expensive prizes, usually won by professional gondoliers. Then there are the coarser revelries associated with the annual Film Festival and the very entertaining public flaps over the mountings of the Biennale, the modern art show that has never failed to generate enough controversy to keep the critics and participants vitriolically at odds with each other in the press for the full twenty-four months between showings. Sandwiched between these major happenings are a great host of lesser manifestations, usually featuring lights, costumes, and music, all rooted in some past occurrence and punctiliously authenticated by the historians of the relentlessly imaginative Ente del Turismo.

The basic idea, of course, is to keep the tourists, with their travellers' checks and credit cards, coming, and not just during the traditional season. About ten years ago, the city administration sponsored a relaunching of the winter carnival, with the appropriate rhetoric to authenticate the proceedings and imbue them with the unique Venetian patina of authenticity. "Everywhere they call it 'carnival,' but everywhere it's different," wrote the anonymous author of the official pamphlet announcing the undertaking. "The carnival is more a 'state of being' than a 'doing.' For this reason, the carnival is the mask, behind which each person conceals his appearance, but through which he reveals himself." Masks have always been a feature of Venice's carnival season, particularly during the last two centuries of the city's decadence, when the upper classes and wealthy foreign visitors disported themselves wantonly behind them, and the canals and *calli* of the Serenissima swarmed with the most expensive courtesans in Europe.

Until the mayor's initiative, the carnival had lapsed into a squalid travesty of itself, featuring small groups of grotesquely made-up children disporting themselves in the larger *campi* and which the poor used as a begging expedition. In 1980, the refurbished proceedings, which lasted for five days, promoted what amounted to an open-air costume ball in Piazza San Marco and a number of cultural manifestations, all connected in some way, however tangential, to the historicity of the Venetian carnival.

Since then, the enterprise has become almost too much of a success. It now lasts eleven days, includes dozens of lectures, concerts, plays, ballets, operas, and art shows, and nightly converts Piazza San Marco into a huge discotheque for as many as forty thousand elaborately costumed and masked revellers. The last Saturday of the celebration lures an estimated one hundred and fifty thousand Italian and foreign visitors into the city, nearly twice the resident population. It has, in other words, become another in the seemingly endless series of public to-dos designed, according to the more cynical observers of the local scene, to keep the tourist cash flowing and at a time of year when Venice is shrouded in cold fogs and has for decades hibernated behind the closed shutters of her hotels and crumbling palazzi.

Despite the cavillers, with their by now familiar complaint that Venice is in more danger of being submerged by tourists than by the capricious waters of her lagoon, there is no doubt that the carnival, like every other festival here, is enjoyed by a majority of the citizens, many of whom take an active part in the proceedings. (One of the secondary benefits has been a revival of the ancient art of the *mascararo*, the designing and making of the sort of elaborate masks that used to be worn for the occasion by the aristocrats of the republic and which are now on sale year-round in many shops as expensive, original souvenirs.) And although the basic thrust of the enterprise is, indeed, to make money, this consideration doesn't seem either to embarrass the Venetians or to diminish their own pleasure in participating. "We can't complain, because, after all, mass tourism was invented by us," a Venetian acquaintance informed me one day. "As for the masks, people used to come to Venice under false identities partly in order not to be stripped of their wealth. We are an island people and islanders have always been pirates."

It is only mildly ironic in this context that the diversion which now arouses the greatest local enthusiasm is the only one almost completely divorced from money-making and which cannot trace its origins back to any specific historical event or religious date. The *vogalonga*, or "long row," was dreamed up in 1974 as a lark by a group of young men, most of whom belonged to one or another of the city's rowing clubs. One of the men, Paolo Rosa Salva, had recently completed his military service in the Alpine troops, who put on a "long march" on skis as part of their training exercises, and he suggested a similar enterprise to his friends. On St. Martin's Day, November 11, nine boats set off for a row across the lagoon and down the length of the Lido to the village of Malamocco, where prizes of salads and chickens were awarded to every participant. "It was not a competition," Rosa Salva recently recalled. "It was a sort of rediscovery of the lagoon."

They had so much fun that they decided to publicize the event and see if they couldn't involve the city in some sort of similar annual affair. The whole history of Venice is inseparably connected to the existence of the lagoon, they reasoned, but in recent years the citizens seemed to have lost touch with this quintessential local aspect of life. "People were going less and less into the lagoon," a journalist for the Venetian daily *Il Gazzettino* recently observed. "The traditional boats were disappearing, replaced by more convenient ones made of plastic." Rosa Salva and his friends saw the *vogalonga* as an opportunity to reawaken enthusiasm for a traditional Venetian pastime, and also as a way of protesting against the increasing presence of speedboats and other noisy motorized forms of transportation in the waters.

To their surprise, the idea caught fire. With the full cooperation of the municipal and maritime authorities,

and the enthusiastic support of *Il Gazzettino*, the first official *vogalonga* was held on May 8, 1975. There had been
worries expressed over how many people would actually
participate and whether the amateur oarsmen would be
able to negotiate a punishing thirty-kilometer route, but
these were soon dispelled. Five hundred and forty-three
pioneer rowers in all kinds of vessels showed up early in
the morning at the broad mouth of the Grand Canal,
between the Riva degli Schiavoni and the island of San
Giorgio, and milled happily about awaiting the start. "It
was like seeing one of those eighteenth-century prints,
with the basin full of wooden boats," an American resident recently recalled. "When the cannon on San Giorgio
went off—boom!—everyone began to row like mad. It
was the greatest thing I ever saw."

The *vogalonga* was an immediate and huge success.
Thirty-six hundred rowers in 1,197 boats took part in the
second edition, held on May 28, 1976, and in 1979 over
five thousand participants in more than seventeen hundred

boats tackled the by now traditional thirty-two kilometer route, which is in the shape of a bulbous eight, from the basin of San Marco around Sant' Elena to Murano, Mazzorbo, Burano, Sant'Erasmo, and back up to the Rio Cannaregio to the Grand Canal. Usually, no more than half the boats complete the course, but no one keeps tabs and no one cares. The *vogalonga* is not a race and it has never been privately sponsored or commercialized. Anyone can row in it, including enthusiasts from other parts of the country and foreigners, more and more of whom are showing up each year. Each rower, whether he finishes the full course or not, receives a "diploma of participation" and a commemorative medal. "The whole point, after all, is to have a good time," my American friend remarked. "It's a celebration, not a contest."

The *vogalonga* I attended a few years ago was no exception. Despite the prospect of a cold and rainy day (according to the forecasters, it had been the worst spring since 1763), 3,389 boats took part. I showed up at the

Riva degli Schiavoni at about eight A.M., an hour before the official starting time, to find dozens of entries already festively milling about in every direction under an ominously gray sky, while recorded Vivaldi blared from loudspeakers mounted in Piazza San Marco.

I counted twenty-two different kinds of vessels, from one-man kayaks and *sandolini* to sleek racing shells and cumbersome rowboats manned by muscular teams of uniformed and helmeted oarsmen, and including, of course, a large sprinkling of gondolas. Several of the latter were crewed by women, who received the loudest cheers from a great crowd of watchers massed along the banks to witness their departure and whose boats were the gayest, some adorned with flowers from stem to stern. At nine o'clock, precisely on the hour, the rowers raised their oars in salute and took off, as the crowd cheered and the cannon on San Giorgio boomed, blowing a white puff of smoke over the extraordinary scene. All around me people were shouting and waving, and, like my American friend, I found myself beaming from the sheer exhilaration induced by the spectacle.

Along with thousands of others, I strolled leisurely across town and found a post just below the Ponte delle Guglie, a bridge over the Rio Cannaregio under which the finishers would have to pass. They began to show up shortly after eleven o'clock and straggled in for several hours—sweaty, exhausted, and triumphant—to the clapping and loud *"bravi"* of the rest of us, packed in like anchovies along the winding banks of the canals, the parapets of the bridges, and the windows and balconies of the palazzi. All of Venice seemed to be present, while, luckily, the rain held off and the sun even managed to break through for a couple of hours.

Among the arrivals were boats I had singled out earlier, as well as many extraordinary ones I hadn't noticed before. My personal favorite was a slow-moving black gondola rowed by a husband-and-wife team in their seventies. The woman, bent with age, was perched on the prow and gazing fiercely straight ahead, with a great hooked beak of a nose that I recognized from a score of Venetian paintings and that reminded me of some warrior doge storming the ramparts of a beleaguered city. She and her husband rowed slowly and in perfect, graceful synchronization. A number of us were happily in tears, without quite knowing why, and it didn't matter in the least that she and her consort had almost certainly rowed no more than a small portion of the route.

I discussed the matter later with Count Girolamo Marcello, a middle-aged Venetian nobleman, who can trace his lineage back to the eighth century, and he maintained that Venice "is only sensations, impressions." The *vogalonga* stirs up ancient emotions of pride and longing deep enough, the count maintained, to make even the most reclusive of the city's surviving aristocrats want to share in the goings-on. When I asked him whether he, too, had participated in the long row, however, he shook his head and smiled. He preferred to watch, he informed me, from a private office inside the Palazzo Ducale. "The Marcellos have never rowed," he explained apologetically. "They have always been in command of the ships."

THE LAGOON HAS been the central preoccupation of Venetian life for about fifteen hundred years, but never more so than in the past two decades, when the city has been increasingly and repeatedly flooded by *acque alte*, or "high waters." Venice rests an average of about thirty inches above sea level on quite literally millions of rock-hard wooden piles driven like stakes over the centuries into the mud. The lagoon itself, which is about thirty-five miles long and never more than seven miles wide, is a crescent-shaped, 210-square-mile shallow body of water full of mud shoals and sandbanks, peppered with partly submerged islands, crisscrossed by narrow, treacherous channels and subject to often capricious currents. From the very beginning, the *acque alte* have been a feature of life here, especially in the late fall and winter, when the warm

African sirocco blows hard enough from the south to push the relatively shallow upper portion of the Adriatic toward its banks. The water pours into the lagoon through the three channel entrances past the Lido, the long sandy reef that protects the city from the open sea, and at high tide surges over the *fondamenta*, floods the canals and bubbles up through the drains of Piazza San Marco and the *campi*. Throughout history Venice has suffered periodic flooding, but never for very long, and the phenomenon was always regarded as the relatively small price the Serenissima had to pay to remain virtually impregnable to attack, thus guaranteeing her independence. *Acqua alta* even became a metaphor for freedom, as in 1848, when Venice rose against the Austrians, briefly restored the republic and sang a song warning the Hapsburgs that "the water is rising around the doors, it will be hard to sponge it away."

Much has been written in recent years, however, about the high waters that now threaten the very survival of the city. During the first fifty years after official records began to be kept, in 1876, Venice was flooded an average of twice a year. During the 1930s, however, the numbers rose, until during the fifties the city was being inundated an average of sixteen times annually. Today, that figure has more than doubled, and it does not include the many other days of the year when Piazza San Marco and its surrounding area, the lowest lying quarter of the city, lie under at least several inches of water for hours at a time. An official *acqua alta* is gauged at three and a half feet above sea level, a height that will flood most of the *centro storico*. When it continues to rise, quite often to four feet and occasionally to five and six feet, the damage to the more ancient buildings and vulnerable art treasures, as well as to basic public services, can be devastating, as in the famous flood of 1966, when the water rose to a level of nearly six and a half feet above sea level and caused havoc.

Except for the worst manifestations, the

Venetians usually seem to be able to cope quite well with this contingency. In the lower-lying portions, they have pretty much abandoned their ground floors, the shopkeepers have improvised waterproof barriers at their front doors and raised their merchandise to higher shelves, and everyone sloshes cheerfully about in rubber boots or tiptoes gingerly along over the raised wooden walkways that crisscross the more frequently flooded areas. Still, no one denies that the problem is a major one. The *acque alte* now afflict the city all year-round. When I was there in May, for instance, a time of year once considered immune, the sirens warning of an impending high water went off twice, the first time at midnight, May 21, which roused people from their beds and sent many of them hurrying to their places of business to take protective measures.

This particular *acqua alta* submerged 70 percent of the city. From my third-story window in San Polo, near the Rialto, I watched the water ooze up over the bank of the canal at the end of my *calle* and silently invade the whole narrow alley, burying it under slimy, refuse-strewn liquid. The harm even such a relatively minor flooding can cause is considerable. "The humidity that creeps up the walls," a reporter recently noted in the weekly *Panorama.* "And the grim, threatening, irresistible, treacherous, cursed water. High water that invades *campi, fondamenti, calli,* hidden gardens, shops, the ground floors of inhabited houses." The walls of many buildings, the writer pointed out, have been permanently marked with dates testifying to the unenviable high-water levels reached during the more damaging episodes, and on others the effect can be traced by the salty encrustations and corrosions the receding waters leave behind. There is little doubt in anyone's mind that, unless some remedy is found, Venice will eventually crumble away and sink permanently beneath the polluted waters of her lagoon.

The trouble can be traced back to the years immediately after the First World War, when a number of private industries began to build factories at Porto

Marghera, a few kilometers west of Venice, on marshland drained and reclaimed from the water. The original idea seemed sound, since Venice had ceased to exist as an important seaport, and it was necessary to create jobs for thousands of people unable to earn a living from tourism; the Veneto in general, a backward agricultural province, had become one of the poorest areas in Italy.

Unfortunately, the cure turned out to be worse than the disease. The development of the industrial zones along the coast, which became frenzied during the late fifties and sixties, lured more and more people into the once quiet residential suburb of Mestre, which became a huge urban sprawl of housing developments, where two hundred and fifty thousand people now live. Every year the population of Venice itself decreased, however, so that today only about eighty thousand citizens still make their homes here. "The fact is that the industrial zone of Venice no longer has anything Venetian about it," Indro Montanelli, the author of a series of articles on the problem, commented in the *Corriere della Sera* in the late sixties. "Not labor, because this is provided not by Venice, but by the land that the peasants have, here as well, abandoned en masse to transform themselves into workers. Not capital, because the firms which have established themselves here have their home bases in Milan and Turin, from where most of their executives and technicians come. . . . What should have been the lung of Venice has become an outpost of the Lombard-Piedmontese economy that squeezes and crushes Venice."

The industries on the mainland require adequate space, and the filled-in land they occupy has greatly reduced the drainage area of the lagoon, causing the tides to back up. Their need for fresh water, which they at first pumped exclusively from underground artesian wells, lowered ground levels. They caused the access channels from the open sea to be dredged in some places to twice their normal depth and excavated an entirely new one to accommodate the larger oil tankers that needed to reach the refineries, measures that tended to increase both the weight and volume of the currents flowing daily in and out through the approaches to the city. They discharged chemicals and untreated waste directly into the lagoon, which altered its delicate ecological balance and ravaged the local fishing industry. (The clouds of gnats that now fill the sky during the summer months are a direct result of the reduced number of fish, which feed on the larvae.) They belched pollutants into the air that have caused marbles, bronzes, even the tough white Istrian stone of which much of the city is built to decay and rot. And as the years have passed, despite repeated acknowledgements from some of the perpetrators and from many persons in positions of authority that there *is* a problem and that something eventually will have to be done; despite the implementation of a few corrective measures (the artesian wells have been shut down and several water purification plants are under construction on the mainland); despite the passage of a special law in 1973 to save Venice and a proposed outlay of over a billion dollars, about a quarter of it already appropriated by the Italian Parliament, to achieve this laudable aim—nothing has been finally decided, no comprehensive program has been put into action, and no basic agreement has even been reached as to how to proceed.

The plan currently in vogue, and the one favored by industry, is to construct huge water gates at the three main entrances to the lagoon, which could be shut against the high tides. This is opposed by most ecologists, as well as many other experts, who claim it won't work, but will simply shift the full weight of the sea elsewhere, perhaps over the Lido itself, while preventing the tides from carrying out their necessary cleansing and renewing functions inside the lagoon. What does seem clear to everyone, however, even the most sanguine optimists, is that the thousand-year-old successful relationship between man and his environment in the Venetian lagoon has been effectively destroyed. According to a local expert named

Marino Potenza, in a recent booklet entitled *Il Mare Era Più Lontano* (The Sea Was Farther Away), the lagoon now revenges itself by swallowing up the city at will, just as easily as the torrents of words devoted to the subject drown out the calls for immediate action. "They hold meetings, studies, seminars, and a tide of paper ends up overwhelming the question," Signor Potenza observes. "A lagoon of chatter, someone called it. But the focal point of the problem is still far off and perhaps it isn't even being approached from the right direction."

The main reason it has been so difficult in Venice to agree on a way to save the city is that the Serenissima is no longer mistress of her own fate. Administratively, Venice includes both Porto Marghera and Mestre, the ugly stepchildren, with their acres of docks, smoke-belching factories, refineries, chemical plants, and hideous apartment complexes. The interests of the mainland residents are necessarily linked to their jobs, and their main concern in recent years has been the financial ups and downs of the

Italian economy. Despite some recent signs of improve-
ment, the local plants and the port are still operating at
far less than capacity and workers are periodically laid off.
In such a climate of potential despair, it is largely useless
to talk as if the only major concern of the area's inhabitants should be the elimination of the *acque alte*, the
restoration of the lagoon and the preservation of Venice
as an open-air museum for foreign tourists. Whatever the
solutions decided upon to save Venice, the interests of the
industrial workers and their families will have to be taken
into account, a consideration that is always uppermost in
the mind of every local politician, in or out of office.
When an attempt was made, in 1979, to separate the
Serenissima as a political entity from Marghera and
Mestre by holding a referendum, the move was opposed
by all of the political parties and was handily defeated.

Tourism, however, is the city's leading industry
and would seem to offer the best hope for the future.
The sheer number of visitors is astonishing. During the

summer months, they pour into the *centro storico* at the rate of between twenty and thirty thousand a day. They pack the ferries and the bridges, swarm over the Rialto and down the Merceria, move in a sludgelike mass through the narrow *calli*, bunch up in line for gondolas and speedboats, elbow each other in the stores and at the trinket counters, squat exhausted in whatever shade they can find in Piazza San Marco and along the banks of the canals. Most of them come for no more than a day or two, many without hotel reservations and carrying all of their belongings on their backs. They spend close to a billion and a half dollars a year and without them Venice would have been reduced by now to a ghost city inhabited by the very old and the canal rats.

Nevertheless, this so-called mass tourism causes difficulties of its own. The campers don't spend enough money, according to the municipal authorities, to pay for the damage they cause, in contributing to the pollution of the waters, the garbage in the streets, the wear and tear on public transport, pavements, and monuments. Several years ago, the problem became so acute that the mayor proposed closing the city to anyone without a room reservation and selling a limited number of daily admission tickets to everyone else. The measure was fiercely opposed by most of his colleagues in the governing coalition, as well as by the tourist bureau, but it was applauded by many Venetians. "Everyone understood my proposal very well," the mayor declared. "Certainly it's an idea and we have to discuss it together." He suggested closing the causeway linking Venice to the mainland to all auto traffic, converting the railway into a mass transit system, with new terminals north and south of the present single facility, and building youth hostels and other campgrounds to absorb the great mass of visitors. He also suggested converting the Arsenal, now a mostly unused military base that occupies one-sixth of the land area of the *centro storico*, into a center for campers and visitors seeking cheap lodgings. "But above all," he continued, "I want to make Venice understood to the tourists. It's not possible they should arrive as barbarians and not even go and see one museum."

This emphasis on what the mayor and his supporters called "quality tourism" led to charges that the administration would like to build a dike of money around Venice and convert the Serenissima into a sort of rich man's Disneyland, admission limited to an elite with enough credit cards to foot the bills. The battle lines on this issue, as on so many others, have been drawn for decades and everyone seems to have his own views on the subject. "We've studied these problems for a hundred years," the owner of a bookstore in San Marco told me one day, "and we do nothing." When I quoted him to another Venetian acquaintance of mine, however, the latter disagreed. "It is not that we do nothing," he said. "If we wish to go forward, however, we have to study our past, because we have had all of these problems before. If we become exasperated, it is because outsiders cannot understand, they are not Venetians. And that is irritating to us."

There is even comfort to be derived, I discovered, from the political gridlock that has immobilized every rescue effort. "Ecology consciousness has been much raised in the past few years," Paolo Rosa Salva informed me one morning, in the local office of Italia Nostra. "Now there are several magazines specializing in the ecology and they are widely read. So the fact that nothing has been done is good, in a way, because at least nothing terrible has been done."

It does seem to outsiders to take the Venetians a very long time to make decisions and to agree to act on anything. The treasures of the Ca' d'Oro, an outstanding example of fifteenth-century Venetian architecture containing a priceless collection of paintings by Mantegna, Guardi, the Bellinis, Titian, and other great masters, were barred to public view for fifteen years because of haggling over bureaucratic procedures and scrambling about for the necessary funds to complete the work. Another recently opened exhibit inside the Palazzo Ducale, for example, also took several years to prepare, even though it provides such a fascinating glimpse into the secret backstage life of the republic that it is possible to wonder what could have taken the authorities so long to get around to mounting it.

Now open to inspection is the hidden warren of small rooms and prison cells, linked by narrow corridors, steep staircases and secret entrances, where the real day-to-day business of the Serenissima was transacted. The formal affairs of state were conducted in the open—in the ducal quarters, the luxurious reception rooms, and the Great Council Chamber familiar to millions of casual visitors—but the dazzling facade hid a humbler and darker reality. Here are the private offices of the secretaries, lawyers, prosecutors, registrars, notaries, and other civil servants; the archives, the kitchens, the storerooms, the arms; the frighteningly intimate chambers where the Council of Ten and the three robed judges of the Holy Inquisition debated the fates of their charges; the torture room, where the wretched suspects were painfully interrogated; the tiny rooftop cells called the Leads, freezing in winter and stifling in summer, where the more eminent prisoners, including Giacomo Casanova, were housed. And throughout, scattered casually over the walls and ceilings of the main halls, can be seen frescoes by Veronese and others, as well as a pair of tremendous triptychs, painted between 1500 and 1505 by Hieronymous Bosch. The tour, by reservation only and limited to groups of no more than twenty-five at a time, has been brilliantly conceived and painstakingly documented; it is an absolutely essential experience to anyone more than casually interested in the terrifying humdrum realities of history.

Not long ago, the Italian publishing house of Longanesi reprinted, forty years after its first appearance, a book entitled *Agenti Segreti a Venezia, 1705-1797* (Secret Agents in Venice), edited by Giovanni Comisso, a scholar who had come across the material while visiting the State Archives of Venice, during the winter of 1940. What he found were the detailed reports and comments submitted by local spies and paid informers of the republic during the last century of its existence. They provided a complete picture, Comisso noted, of "Venetian life in the seventeen-hundreds, with so many tiny and gossipy particulars as to supply what amounted to a photographic documentation, even in color, of life during that period."

The book, with its depiction of a decadent police state and its host of lickspittles, soon ran into trouble with the Fascist censors, but it has been reissued several times and has now become a minor classic of its kind. This is because the people recruited by the state inquisitors to keep tabs on their fellow citizens were not professionals, but simply local hangers-on, most of whom had nothing better to do with their time than gossip colorfully and viciously about their neighbors. One of them, for a time, was Giacomo Casanova, who, at the end of his life—old, tired, and starving—humbly offered his paid services. His reports are characterized by an excess of unctuous moralizing on the scandalous behavior of his compatriots, but apparently the Venetian magistrates read them with a distrustful eye. Casanova was himself simultaneously spied upon and the pages devoted to his activities reveal him as an impenitent heretic, still devoted to seduction and the gaming tables.

The Serenissima recruited her informers from every stratum of society in every quarter of the city and nothing escaped their vigilant senses. No detail, no incident, no compromising phrase went unnoted. Every major and minor transgression is reported, with illuminating comments on appearance, behavior, expressions, tones of voice, gestures, postures, circumstances, all the details to make up a series of the sort of delicious genre pictures painted by Pietro Longhi. As the years passed and the republic sank further and further into inertia, decadence, and squalor, with the Jacobin winds already blowing coldly through the *calli* and Napoleon looming larger in the background of the city's long, last *carnevale*, the inquisitive, brilliant, witty, malicious, fascinating

Venetians kept right on sticking their noses into each other's business and talking, talking, talking. Luckily for the rest of us, they have never stopped.

Lady Anna Miller

VENETIAN LADIES AND THEIR
CAVALIERI SERVENTI

THE CUSTOM OF *Cavalieri Serventi* prevails universally here: this usage would appear in a proper light, and take off a great part of the odium thrown upon the Italians, if the *Cavalieri Serventi* were called husbands; for the real husband, or beloved friend, of a Venetian lady (often for life), is the *Cicisbeo*. The husband married in Church is the choice of her friends, not by any means of the lady. . . .

The Venetian ladies have a gay manner of dress-

English socialite and heiress Lady Anna Miller traveled widely and, on occasion, dabbled in writing. This is from the no-holds-barred Letters from Italy, *published anonymously in 1776.*

ing their heads, which becomes them extremely when young, but appears very absurd when age has furrowed over their fine skins, and brought them almost to the ground. I felt a shock at first sight of a tottering old pair I saw enter a coffee-house the other evening; they were both shaking with the palsy, leant upon each other, and supported themselves by a crutch-stick; they were bent almost double by the weight of years and infirmities, yet the lady's head was dressed with great care; a little rose-coloured hat, nicely trimmed with blond, was stuck just above her right ear, and over her left was a small mat of artificial flowers; her few grey hairs behind were tied with ribbon, but so thinly scattered over her forehead, that large patches of her shrivelled skin appeared between the parting curls; the *Cavaliere* was not dressed in the same style, all his elegance consisted in an abundance of wig which flowed upon his shoulders. I enquired who this venerable couple were, and learnt, that the gentleman had been the faithful *Cavaliere* of the same lady above forty years; that they had regularly frequented the Place of St. Mark and the coffee-houses, and with the most steady constancy had loved each other, till age and disease were conducting them hand in hand together to the grave.

Casanova

VENETIAN YEARS

AT THE END of January, finding myself under the necessity of procuring two hundred sequins, Madame Manzoni contrived to obtain for me from another woman the loan of a diamond ring worth five hundred. I made up my mind to go to Treviso, fifteen miles distant from Venice, to pawn the ring at the Mont-de-pieté, which there lends money upon valuables at the rate of five per-

---

The notorious Venetian "adventurer" Giovanni Jacopo Casanova stalked the great capitals of Europe, making his way alternately as a charlatan, gambler, preacher, and, of course, seducer. Our hero is in top form in this gondola rendezvous (circa 1760) from book 1 of his 12-volume Memoires.

cent. That useful establishment does not exist in Venice, where the Jews have always managed to keep the monopoly in their hands.

I got up early one morning, and walked to the end of the *canale regio*, intending to engage a gondola to take me as far as Mestra, where I could take post horses, reach Treviso in less than two hours, pledge my diamond ring, and return to Venice the same evening.

As I passed along St. Job's Quay, I saw in a two-oared gondola a country girl beautifully dressed. I stopped to look at her; the gondoliers, supposing that I wanted an opportunity of reaching Mestra at a cheap rate, rowed back to the shore.

Observing the lovely face of the young girl, I do not hesitate, but jump into the gondola, and pay double fare, on condition that no more passengers are taken. An elderly priest was seated near the young girl, he rises to let me take his place, but I politely insist upon his keeping it.

"Those gondoliers," said the elderly priest, addressing me in order to begin the conversation, "are very fortunate. They took us up at the Rialto for thirty soldi, on condition that they would be allowed to embark other passengers, and here is one already; they will certainly find more."

"When I am in a gondola, reverend sir, there is no room left for any more passengers."

So saying, I give forty more soldi to the gondoliers, who, highly pleased with my generosity, thank me and call me excellency. The good priest, accepting that title as truly belonging to me, entreats my pardon for not having addressed me as such.

"I am not a Venetian nobleman, reverend sir, and I have no right to the title of *Eccellenza*."

"Ah!" says the young lady, "I am very glad of it."

"Why so, signora?"

"Because when I find myself near a nobleman I am afraid. But I suppose that you are an *illustrissimo*."

"Not even that, signora; I am only an advocate's clerk."

"So much the better, for I like to be in the company of persons who do not think themselves above me. My father was a farmer, brother of my uncle here, rector of P——, where I was born and bred. As I am an only daughter I inherited my father's property after his death, and I shall likewise be heiress to my mother, who has been ill a long time and cannot live much longer which causes me a great deal of sorrow; but it is the doctor who says it. Now, to return to my subject, I do not suppose that there is much difference between an advocate's clerk and the daughter of a rich farmer. I only say so for the sake of saying something, for I know very well that, in travelling, one must accept all sorts of companions: is it not so, uncle?"

"Yes, my dear Christine, and as proof you see that this gentleman has accepted our company without knowing who or what we are."

"But do you think I would have come if I had not been attracted by the beauty of your lovely niece?"

At these words the good people burst out laughing. As I did not think that there was anything very cunning in what I had said, I judged that my travelling companions were rather simple, and I was not sorry to find them so.

"Why do you laugh so heartily, beautiful *demigella?* Is it to shew me your fine teeth? I confess that I have never seen such a splendid set in Venice."

"Oh! it is not for that, sir, although everyone in Venice has paid me the same compliment. I can assure you that in P— all the girls have teeth as fine as mine. Is it not a fact, uncle?"

"Yes, my dear niece."

"I was laughing, sir, at a thing which I will never tell you."

"Oh! tell me, I entreat you."

"Oh! certainly not, never."

"I will tell you myself," says the curate.

"You will not," she exclaims, knitting her beautiful eyebrows. "If you do I will go away."

"I defy you to do it, my dear. Do you know what she said, sir, when she saw you on the wharf? 'Here is a very handsome young man who is looking at me, and would not be sorry to be with us.' And when she saw that the gondoliers were putting back for you to embark she was delighted."

While the uncle was speaking to me, the indignant niece was slapping him on the shoulder.

"Why are you angry, lovely Christine, at my hearing that you liked my appearance, when I am so glad to let you know how truly charming I think you?"

"You are glad for a moment. Oh! I know the Venetians thoroughly now. They have all told me that they were charmed with me, and not one of those I would have liked ever made a declaration to me."

"What sort of declaration did you want?"

"There's only one sort for me, sir; the declaration leading to a good marriage in church, in the sight of all men. Yet we remained a fortnight in Venice; did we not, uncle?"

"This girl," said the uncle, "is a good match, for she possesses three thousand crowns. She has always said that she would marry only a Venetian, and I have accompanied her to Venice to give her an opportunity of being known. A worthy woman gave us hospitality for a fortnight, and has presented my niece in several houses where she made the acquaintance of marriageable young men, but those who pleased her would not hear of marriage, and those who would have been glad to marry her did not take her fancy."

"But do you imagine, reverend sir, that marriages can be made like omelets? A fortnight in Venice, that is nothing; you ought to live there at least six months. Now, for instance, I think your niece sweetly pretty, and I should consider myself fortunate if the wife whom God intends for me were like her, but, even if she offered me now a dowry of fifty thousand crowns on condition that our wedding takes place immediately, I would refuse her. A prudent young man wants to know the character of a girl before he marries her, for it is neither money nor beauty which can ensure happiness in married life."

"What do you mean by character?" asked Christine; "is it a beautiful hand-writing?"

"No, my dear. I mean the qualities of the mind and the heart. I shall most likely get married sometime, and I have been looking for a wife for the last three years, but I am still looking in vain. I have known several young girls almost as lovely as you are, and all with a good marriage portion, but after an acquaintance of two or three months I found out that they could not make me happy."

"In what were they deficient?"

"Well, I will tell you, because you are not acquainted with them, and there can be no indiscretion on my part. One whom I certainly would have married, for I loved her dearly, was extremely vain. She would have ruined me in fashionable clothes and by her love for luxuries. Fancy! she was in the habit of paying one sequin every month to the hair-dresser, and as much at least for pomatum and perfumes."

"She was a giddy, foolish girl. Now, I spend only ten soldi in one year on wax which I mix with goat's grease, and there I have an excellent pomatum."

"Another, whom I would have married two years ago, laboured under a disease which would have made me unhappy; as soon as I knew of it, I ceased my visits."

"What disease was it?"

"A disease which would have prevented her from being a mother, and, if I get married, I wish to have children."

"All that is in God's hands, but I know that my health is excellent. Is it not, uncle?"

"Another was too devout, and that does not suit

me. She was so over-scrupulous that she was in the habit of going to her confessor twice a week, and every time her confession lasted at least one hour. I want my wife to be a good Christian, but not bigoted."

"She must have been a great sinner, or else she was very foolish. I confess only once a month, and get through everything in two minutes. Is it not true, uncle? and if you were to ask me any questions, uncle, I should not know what more to say."

"One young lady thought herself more learned than I, although she would, every minute, utter some absurdity. Another was always low-spirited, and my wife must be cheerful."

"Hark to that, uncle! You and my mother are always chiding me for my cheerfulness."

"Another, whom I did not court long, was always afraid of being alone with me, and if I gave her a kiss she would run and tell her mother."

"How silly she must have been! I have never yet

listened to a lover, for we have only rude peasants in P——, but I know very well that there are some things which I would not tell my mother."

"One had a rank breath; another painted her face, and, indeed, almost every young girl is guilty of that fault. I am afraid marriage is out of the question for me, because I want, for instance, my wife to have black eyes, and in our days almost every woman colours them by art; but I cannot be deceived, for I am a good judge."

"Are mine black?"

"Ah! Ah!"

"You are laughing?"

"I laugh because your eyes certainly appear to be black, but they are not so in reality. Never mind, you are very charming in spite of that."

"Now, that is amusing. You pretend to be a good judge, yet you say that my eyes are dyed black. My eyes, sir, whether beautiful or ugly, are now the same as God made them. Is it not so, uncle?"

"I never had any doubt of it, my dear niece."

"And you do not believe me, sir?"

"No, they are too beautiful for me to believe them natural."

"Oh, dear me! I cannot bear it."

"Excuse me, my lovely *damigella*, I am afraid I have been too sincere."

After that quarrel we remained silent. The good curate smiled now and then, but his niece found it very hard to keep down her sorrow.

At intervals I stole a look at her face, and could see that she was very near crying. I felt sorry, for she was a charming girl. In her hair, dressed in the fashion of wealthy countrywomen, she had more than one hundred sequins' worth of gold pins and arrows which fastened the plaits of her long locks as dark as ebony. Heavy gold earrings, and a long chain, which was wound twenty times round her snowy neck, made a fine contrast to her complexion, on which lilies and the roses were admirably blended. It was the first time that I had seen a country beauty in such splendid apparel. Six years before, Lucie at Paséan had captivated me, but in a different manner.

Christine did not utter a single word, she was in despair, for her eyes were truly of the greatest beauty, and I was cruel enough to attack them. She evidently hated me, and her anger alone kept back her tears. Yet I would not undeceive her, for I wanted her to bring matters to a climax.

When the gondola had entered the long canal of Marghera, I asked the clergyman whether he had a carriage to go to Treviso, through which place he had to pass to reach P—.

"I intended to walk," said the worthy man, "for my parish is poor and I am the same, but I will try to obtain a place for Christine in some carriage travelling that way."

"You would confer a real kindness on me if you would both accept a seat in my chaise; it holds four persons, and there is plenty of room."

"It is a good fortune which we were far from expecting."

"Not at all, uncle; I will not go with this gentleman."

"Why not, my dear niece?"

"Because I will not."

"Such is the way," I remarked, without looking at her, "that sincerity is generally rewarded."

"Sincerity, sir! nothing of the sort," she exclaimed, angrily, "it is sheer wickedness. There can be no true black eyes now for you in the world, but, as you like them, I am very glad of it."

"You are mistaken, lovely Christine, for I have the means of ascertaining the truth."

"What means?"

"Only to wash the eyes with a little lukewarm rosewater; or if the lady cries, the artificial colour is certain to be washed off."

At those words, the scene changed as if by the wand of a conjuror. The face of the charming girl, which had expressed nothing but indignation, spite and disdain, took an air of contentment and of placidity delightful to witness. She smiled at her uncle who was much pleased with the change in her countenance, for the offer of the carriage had gone to his heart.

"Now you had better cry a little, my dear niece, and *il signore* will render full justice to your eyes."

Christine cried in reality, but it was immoderate laughter that made her tears flow.

That species of natural originality pleased me greatly, and as we were going up the steps at the landing-place, I offered her my full apologies; she accepted the carriage. I ordered breakfast, and told a *vetturino* to get a very handsome chaise ready while we had our meal, but the curate said that he must first of all go and say his mass.

"Very well, reverend sir, we will hear it, and you must say it for my intention."

I put a silver ducat in his hand.

"It is what I am in the habit of giving," I observed.

My generosity surprised him so much that he wanted to kiss my hand. We proceeded towards the church, and I offered my arm to the niece who, not knowing whether she ought to accept it or not, said to me,—

"Do you suppose that I cannot walk alone?"

"I have no such idea, but if I do not give you my arm, people will think me wanting in politeness."

"Well, I will take it. But now that I have your arm, what will people think?"

"Perhaps that we love each other and that we make a very nice couple."

"And if anyone should inform your mistress that we are in love with each other, or even that you have given your arm to a young girl?"

"I have no mistress, and I shall have none in

future, because I could not find a girl as pretty as you in all Venice."

"I am very sorry for you, for we cannot go again to Venice; and even if we could, how could we remain there six months? You said that six months were necessary to know a girl well."

"I would willingly defray all your expenses."

"Indeed? Then say so to my uncle, and he will think it over, for I could not go alone."

"In six months you would know me likewise."

"Oh! I know you very well already."

"Could you accept a man like me?"

"Why not?"

"And will you love me?"

"Yes, very much, when you are my husband."

I looked at the young girl with astonishment. She seemed to me a princess in the disguise of a peasant girl. Her dress, made of *gros de Tours* and all embroidered in gold, was very handsome, and cost certainly twice as much as the finest dress of a Venetian lady. Her bracelets, matching the neckchain, completed her rich toilet. She had the figure of a nymph, and the new fashion of wearing a mantle not having yet reached her village, I could see the most magnificent bosom, although her dress was fastened up to the neck. The end of the richly-embroidered skirt did not go lower than the ankles, which allowed me to admire the neatest little foot and the lower part of an exquisitely moulded leg. Her firm and easy walk, the natural freedom of all her movements, a charming look which seemed to say, "I am very glad that you think me pretty," everything, in short, caused the ardent fire of amorous desires to circulate through my veins. I could not conceive how such a lovely girl could have spent a fortnight in Venice without finding a man to marry or to deceive her. I was particularly delighted with her simple, artless way of talking, which in the city might have been taken for silliness.

Absorbed in my thoughts, and having resolved in

my own mind on rendering brilliant homage to her charms, I waited impatiently for the end of the mass.

After breakfast I had great difficulty in convincing the curate that my seat in the carriage was the last one, but I found it easier to persuade him on our arrival in Treviso to remain for dinner and for supper at a small, unfrequented inn, as I took all the expense upon myself. He accepted very willingly when I added that immediately after supper a carriage would be in readiness to convey him to P——, where he would arrive in an hour after a pleasant journey by moonlight. He had nothing to hurry him on, except his wish to say mass in his own church the next morning.

I ordered a fire and a good dinner, and the idea struck me that the curate himself might pledge the ring for me, and thus give me the opportunity of a short interview with his niece. I proposed it to him, saying that I could not very well go myself, as I did not wish to be known. He undertook the commission at once, expressing his pleasure at doing something to oblige me.

He left us, and I remained alone with Christine. I spent an hour with her without trying to give her even a kiss, although I was dying to do so, but I prepared her heart to burn with the same desires which were already burning in me by those words which so easily inflame the imagination of a young girl.

The curate came back and returned me the ring, saying that it could not be pledged until the day after the morrow, in consequence of the Festival of the Holy Virgin. He had spoken to the cashier, who had stated that if I liked the bank would lend double the sum I had asked.

"My dear sir," I said, "you would greatly oblige me if you would come back here from P— to pledge the ring yourself. Now that it has been offered once by you, it might look very strange if it were brought by another person. Of course I will pay all your expenses."

"I promise you to come back."

I hoped he would bring his niece with him.

I was seated opposite to Christine during the dinner, and discovered fresh charms in her every minute, but, fearing I might lose her confidence if I tried to obtain some slight favour, I made up my mind not to go to work too quickly, and to contrive that the curate should take her again to Venice. I thought that there only I could manage to bring love into play and to give to it the food it requires.

"Reverend sir," I said, "let me advise you to take your niece again to Venice. I undertake to defray all expenses, and to find an honest woman with whom your Christine will be as safe as with her own mother. I want to know her well in order to make her my wife, and if she comes to Venice our marriage is certain."

"Sir, I will bring my niece myself to Venice as soon as you inform me that you have found a worthy woman with whom I can leave her in safety."

While we were talking I kept looking at

Christine, and I could see her smile with contentment.

"My dear Christine," I said, "within a week I shall have arranged the affair. In the meantime, I will write to you. I hope that you have no objection to correspond with me."

"My uncle will write for me, for I have never been taught writing."

"What, my dear child! you wish to become the wife of a Venetian, and you cannot write."

"Is it then necessary to know how to write in order to become a wife? I can read well."

"That is not enough, and although a girl can be a wife and a mother without knowing how to trace one letter, it is generally admitted that a young girl ought to be able to write. I wonder you never learned."

"There is no wonder in that, for not one girl in our village can do it. Ask my uncle."

"It is perfectly true, but there is not one who thinks of getting married in Venice, and as you wish for a

Venetian husband you must learn."

"Certainly," I said, "and before you come to Venice, for everybody would laugh at you, if you could not write. I see that it makes you sad, my dear, but it cannot be helped."

"I am sad, because I cannot learn writing in a week."

"I undertake," said her uncle, "to teach you in a fortnight, if you will only practice diligently. You will then know enough to be able to improve by your own exertions."

"It is a great undertaking, but I accept it; I promise you to work night and day, and to begin to-morrow."

After dinner, I advised the priest not to leave that evening, to rest during the night, and I observed that, by going away before day-break, he would reach P— in good time, and feel all the better for it. I made the same proposal to him in the evening, and when he saw that his niece was sleepy, he was easily persuaded to remain. I called for the innkeeper, ordered a carriage for the clergyman, and desired that a fire might be lit for me in the next room where I would sleep, but the good priest said that it was unnecessary, because there were two large beds in our room, that one would be for me and the other for him and his niece.

"We need not undress," he added, "as we mean to leave very early, but you can take off your clothes, sir, because you are not going with us, and you will like to remain in bed to-morrow morning."

"Oh!" remarked Christine, "I must undress myself, otherwise I could not sleep, but I only want a few minutes to get ready in the morning."

I said nothing, but I was amazed. Christine then, lovely and charming enough to wreck the chastity of a Xenocrates, would sleep naked with her uncle! True, he was old, devout, and without any of the ideas which might render such a position dangerous, yet the priest was a man, he had evidently felt like all men, and he ought to have known the danger he was exposing himself to. My carnal-mindedness could not realize such a state of innocence. But it was truly innocent, so much so that he did it openly, and did not suppose that anyone could see anything wrong in it. I saw it all plainly, but I was not accustomed to such things, and felt lost in wonderment. As I advanced in age and in experience, I have seen the same custom established in many countries amongst honest people whose good morals were in no way debased by it, but it was amongst good people, and I do not pretend to belong to that worthy class.

We had had no meat for dinner, and my delicate palate was not over-satisfied. I went down to the kitchen myself, and I told the landlady that I wanted the best that could be procured in Treviso for supper, particularly in wines.

"If you do not mind the expense, sir, trust to me, and I undertake to please you. I will give you some

Gatta wine."

"All right, but let us have supper early."

When I returned to our room, I found Christine caressing the cheeks of her old uncle, who was laughing; the good man was seventy-five years old.

"Do you know what is the matter?" he said to me; "my niece is caressing me because she wants me to leave her here until my return. She tells me that you were like brother and sister during the hour you have spent alone together this morning, and I believe it, but she does not consider that she would be a great trouble to you."

"Not at all, quite the reverse, she will afford me great pleasure, for I think her very charming. As to our mutual behavior, I believe you can trust us both to do our duty."

"I have no doubt of it. Well, I will leave her under your care until the day after to-morrow. I will come back early in the morning so as to attend to your business."

This extraordinary and unexpected arrangement

caused the blood to rush to my head with such violence that my nose bled profusely for a quarter of an hour. It did not frighten me, because I was used to such accidents, but the good priest was in a great fright, thinking that it was a serious hemorrhage.

When I had allayed his anxiety, he left us on some business of his own, saying that he would return at night-fall. I remained alone with the charming, artless Christine, and lost no time in thanking her for the confidence she placed in me.

"I can assure you," she said, "that I wish you to have a thorough knowledge of me; you will see that I have none of the faults which have displeased you so much in the young ladies you have known in Venice, and I promise to learn writing immediately."

"You are charming and true; but you must be discreet in P——, and confide to no one that we have entered into an agreement with each other. You must act according to your uncle's instructions, for it is to him that

I intend to write to make all arrangements."

"You may rely upon my discretion. I will not say anything even to my mother, until you give me permission to do so."

I passed the afternoon, in denying myself even the slightest liberties with my lovely companion, but falling every minute deeper in love with her. I told her a few love stories which I veiled sufficiently not to shock her modesty. She felt interested, and I could see that, although she did not always understand, she pretended to do so, in order not to appear ignorant.

When her uncle returned, I had arranged everything in my mind to make her my wife, and I resolved on placing her, during her stay in Venice, in the house of the same honest widow with whom I had found a lodging for my beautiful Countess A— S—.

We had a delicious supper. I had to teach Christine how to eat oysters and truffles, which she then saw for the first time. Gatta wine is like champagne, it causes merriment without intoxicating, but it cannot be kept for more than one year. We went to bed before midnight, and it was broad daylight when I awoke. The curate had left the room so quietly that I had not heard him.

I looked towards the other bed, Christine was asleep. I wished her good morning, she opened her eyes, and leaning on her elbow, she smiled sweetly.

"My uncle has gone. I did not hear him."

"Dearest Christine, you are as lovely as one of God's angels. I have a great longing to give you a kiss."

"If you long for a kiss, my dear friend, come and give me one."

I jumped out of my bed, decency makes her hide her face. It was cold, and I was in love. I find myself in her arms by one of those spontaneous movements which sentiment alone can cause, and we belong to each other without having thought of it, she happy and rather confused, I delighted, yet unable to realize the truth of a victory won without any contest.

An hour passed in the midst of happiness, during which we forgot the whole world. Calm followed the stormy gusts of passionate love, and we gazed at each other without speaking.

Christine was the first to break the silence:

"What have we done?" she said, softly and lovingly.

"We have become husband and wife."

"What will my uncle say to-morrow?"

"He need not know anything about it until he gives us the nuptial benediction in his own church."

"And when will he do so?"

"As soon as we have completed all the arrangements necessary for a public marriage."

"How long will that be?"

"About a month."

"We cannot be married during Lent."

"I will obtain permission."

"You are not deceiving me?"

"No, for I adore you."

"Then, you no longer want to know me better?"

"No, I know you thoroughly now, and I feel certain that you will make me happy."

"And will you make me happy, too?"

"I hope so."

Marcel Proust

THE FUGITIVE

IT WAS THIS Venice that I used often to explore in the afternoon, when I did not go out with my mother. The fact was that it was easier to find there women of the people, matchsellers, pearl-stringers, glass or lace makers, young seamstresses in black shawls with long fringes, whom there was nothing to prevent me from loving,

French novelist Marcel Proust had his first debilitating attack of asthma in 1880, at age nine. The continuing illness forced the writer into virtual seclusion in his famous "cork lined room." From there he rarely stirred, concentrating solely on what was to become his life's work: the behemoth, minutely detailed Remembrance of Things Past. The Fugitive *is drawn from the first of the seven massive volumes.*

because I had to a large extent forgotten Albertine, and who seemed to me more desirable than others, because I still remembered her a little. Who, in any case, could have told me precisely, in this passionate quest of mine for Venetian women, how much there was of themselves, how much of Albertine, how much of my old, long-cherished desire to visit Venice? Our slightest desire, though unique as a chord, nevertheless includes the fundamental notes on which the whole of our life is built. And sometimes, if we were to eliminate one of them, even one that we do not hear, that we are not aware of, one that has no connection with the object of our quest, we would nevertheless see our whole desire for that object disappear. There were many things that I made no attempt to identify in the excitement I felt as I went in search of Venetian women.

My gondola followed the course of the small canals; like the mysterious hand of a genie leading me through the maze of this oriental city, they seemed, as I advanced, to be cutting a path for me through the heart of a crowded quarter which they bisected, barely parting, with a slender furrow arbitrarily traced, the tall houses with their tiny Moorish windows; and as though the magic guide had been holding a candle in his hand and were lighting the way for me, they kept casting ahead of them a ray of sunlight for which they cleared a route. One felt that between the mean dwellings which the canal had just parted, and which otherwise would have formed a compact whole, no open space had been reserved; so that a campanile or a garden trellis vertically overhung the *rio*, as in a flooded city. But, for both churches and gardens, thanks to the same transposition as in the Grand Canal, the sea so readily served as means of communication, as substitute for street or alley, that on either side of the *canaletto* the belfries rose from the water in this poor and populous district like those of humble and much-frequented parish churches bearing the stamp of their necessity, of their use by crowds of simple folk, the gardens traversed by the canal cutting trailed their startled leaves and fruit in the water, and on the ledges of the houses whose crudely cut stone was still rough as though it had only just been sawn, urchins surprised by the gondola sat back trying to keep their balance and allowing their legs to dangle vertically, like sailors seated upon a swing-bridge the two halves of which have been swung apart, allowing the sea to pass between them. Now and again would appear a handsomer building that happened to be there like a surprise in a box which one has just opened, a little ivory temple with its Corinthian columns and an allegorical statue on its pediment, somewhat out of place among the ordinary surroundings in the midst of which the peristyle with which the canal had provided it retained the look of a landing-stage for market gardeners.

I returned on foot through narrow lanes; I accosted plebeian girls as Albertine perhaps had done, and I should have liked to have her with me. Yet these could not be the same girls; at the time when Albertine had been in Venice, they would have been children still. But, after having been unfaithful in the past, in a basic sense and out of cowardice, to each of the desires that I had conceived as unique—since I had sought an analogous object and not the same one, which I despaired of finding again—now I systematically sought women whom Albertine had not known, just as I no longer sought those that I had desired in the past. True, it often happened to me to recall, with an extraordinary violence of desire, some wench of Méséglise or Paris, of the milk-girl I had seen early in the morning at the foot of a hill during my first journey to Balbec. But alas! I remembered them as they were then, that is to say as they certainly would not be now. So that if in the past I had been led to qualify my impression of the uniqueness of a desire by seeking, in place of a convent-girl I had lost sight of, a similar convent-girl, now, in order to recapture the girls who had troubled my adolescence or that of Albertine, I had to consent to a further departure from the principle of the individuality of desire: what I must look for was not those who were sixteen then, but those who were sixteen to-day, for now, in the absence of that which was most distinctive in the person and which eluded me, what I loved was youth. I knew that the youth of those I had known existed no longer save in my impassioned recollection, and that it was not them, however anxious I might be to make contact with them when my memory recalled them to me, that I must cull if I really wished to harvest the youth and the blossom of the year.

John Ruskin

THE STONES OF VENICE

SINCE THE FIRST dominion of men was asserted over the ocean, three thrones, of mark beyond all others, have been set upon its sands: the thrones of Tyre, Venice, and England. Of the First of these great powers only the memory remains; of the Second, the ruin; the Third, which inherits their greatness, if it forget their

---

John Ruskin was the top art critic of his time, championing a "moral perception of beauty"—as opposed to a sensual one. In 1851, he published the monstrous 3-volume set The Stones of Venice, *an incredibly detailed study of the decadence of the city, as evident in its Gothic architecture. This excerpt is from the introduction.*

example, may be led through prouder eminence to less pitied destruction.

The exaltation, the sin, and the punishment of Tyre have been recorded for us, in perhaps the most touching words ever uttered by the Prophets of Israel against the cities of the stranger. But we read them as a lovely song; and close our ears to the sternness of their warning: for the very depth of the Fall of Tyre has blinded us to its reality, and we forget, as we watch the bleaching of the rocks between the sunshine and the sea, that they were once "as in Eden, the garden of God."

Her successor, like her in perfection of beauty, though less in endurance of dominion, is still left for our beholding in the final period of her decline: a ghost upon the sands of the sea, so weak—so quiet,—so bereft of all but her loveliness, that we might well doubt, as we watched her faint reflection in the mirage of the lagoon, which was the City, and which the Shadow.

I would endeavor to trace the lines of this image

before it be for ever lost, and to record, as far as I may, the warning which seems to me to be uttered by every one of the fast-gaining waves, that beat, like passing bells, against the stones of Venice.

Orson Welles

CHURCHILL IN VENICE

ONE TIME I am in Venice trying to promote some money from a crazy Russian; we're at the Excelsior Hotel on the Lido. Churchill had been voted out of office and is there with Clemmie, and they're together just sitting at a table in the restaurant. And as I came in, for some reason, there was all this Italian gafuffle: "Hello—" "Here

---

In 1941, at the age of 26, George Orson Welles directed the profound, groundbreaking Citizen Kane, *considered by many the greatest film in the history of cinema. The wunderkind never completed another movie to his liking, though, citing massive studio interference. In 1956, Welles was filming* Othello *in Venice and bumped into Winston Churchill.*

he comes——" And as I passed Churchill's table, I bowed to him. And Churchill——I don't know why, for reasons of irony, to send me up, I can't imagine why——half stood up, bowed, and sat down. I suppose it was some kind of joke. Well, the Russian afterward said, "You're close to Churchill," and the deal was closed right there. So the next day I'm swimming, and on the beach I find myself next to Mr. Churchill. And I said, "Mr. Churchill, you don't know what you did for me. By acknowledging my greeting that way, I've got the money for my picture—— settled the whole thing."

All right. Finished swimming. That night, at dinner, we came in again. Churchill *stood up!* And for the rest of the time we were in Venice, every time I came in the restaurant, he *stood* when I passed! Thinking, you know, "Get some money for him." And no matter who I was with——somebody I *couldn't* get any money from——he stood. And people said, "What is this? Every time Churchill sees this actor, this great man——the greatest living fellow—is standing up!" And he thought, "Well, every time I stand up, he gets some more dough—so why not?" Oh God, what a wonderful man he was. And then, the same season, there was the great Bestigui Ball in Venice, where everybody's invited. And I happened to be invited, and of course Churchill was, too, but he was hoping to get back into office and everybody was attacking the ball as conspicuous luxury and all that, so he couldn't go. And here we are all going off in our speed-boats to the ball, and there was Churchill down at the end of the dock watching us leave, ready—and miserable. . . . He would have come dressed as anything, you know, but he just couldn't go. Miserable!

Ezra Pound

VENICE LETTER

Dearest:

Here after divers troubles by land & sea, behold us. It is now about 9:30 A.M. I spent last night in a pic-

---

Ezra Pound had an enormous influence on modern literature, starting scads of magazines and finding publishers for young writers such as T. S. Eliot, Joyce, Hemingway and Marianne Moore. It was in Paris that Pound began his own epic poem, The Cantos, a diatribe against war and commercialism in art. In his later years, he moved to Italy and, shockingly, embraced Mussolini and Fascism.

turesque lodging sul Canal Grande, with a vista of nearly everything, but arose with a firm conviction that I would not spend another night in the same locality. This I have accomplished at a net loss of 3 lire which is fairly good considering I'd paid a week in advance. The signora had *mai visto una persona tanto dispiaciuta*, and to my certain knowledge *no* other Venetian has ever restored cash once rec'd.——on any ground whatever. I've now a tile roof & sun and a small canal, so even the picturesque has not been wholly sacrificed.

At 3 A.M. I thoroughly detested travel. I couldn't tell which I hated worse, travel or the stupid & defenceless condition that one gets into when one stays in the same place & is served hand & foot, videlicit Ch.W. [Church Walk] & Sirmione. The last is too cushioned, tho' the food is not what it might be. They say *'stia sempre nella memoria'*, so I must have paid them too much—No, I won't say that the whole staff was/were *gentile* & even Cracco [the proprietor] whom I detest redeemed himself by telling *Come si fece la donna.*

> Jesu Christo stando nel paradiso terrestre
> pensando come fare compagna d'Adamo—

it needs gestures but you shall have it later.

This place has a cuisine as THEY [CHARS] happen to know, for we dined here yesterday (& lunched before that). The first orzzo in 5 years, and this A.M. positively the 1st cup of coffee that I have ever had in Italy.

The country is looking up—what with Marinetti & the war with Tripoli etc. Venice seemed yesterday like one large Carlton Hotel. I have ordered delicate trousers, & bought gloves that are I fear more ornate than durable. In fact I may say that yesterday was unsullied by any sort of economy.

R & H. [Richard Aldington & Hilda Doolittle] appear to be falling in love with each other somewhere en route from Napoli. I suppose I'll have to be ready with a pontifical sanction & then try to soothe their respective progenitors—at least their communications are *very* vague.

My last wooing of the sun & the lago was so violent that I've very nearly got a whole new hide, which is worse than getting new raiment—it is more economical in one way, but it devours one's time. Anyhow I arise on this the 3rd day of Maggio [May]—or rather arose some hours since & was brought hither by swift oarsmen—but am now soothed & at peace & feel ages wiser and more mature than I did 24 hours ago. Yesterday, also, I saw one gondola crawl about six feet over another gondola's middle. I've never seen anything of the sort before—New Italy! cosa di Sport! etc.—still it produced the same antique mode of eloquence so I suppose there is a conservative principle somewhere.

That 'Faun' thing is no good—don't worry about criticizing it—or rather do—go ahead & see if you can diagnose it.

On the whole mi piace Venezia. I felt that way

when I arrived & despite the uneven fortunes I am restored to the belief, even in the absence of the two people who in all decency ought to regard it as their sole duty to stand present & keep me amused. If not, why have I reared them with such persistent solicitude—You had much better do your sketching here—& Horatio Brown might be persuaded to "instruct" you. God!! hast ever seen an opus Brownensis!?!!?!

Ebbène its a charming morning, aura dolce, just enough to flutter my papers without being a d——d nuisance. I go forth seeking mail, c/o Tho. Cook, as I scribbled on the back of my last envelope.

Dieu te garde et le bon soleil.

E.

Edith Wharton

ITALIAN BACKGROUNDS

IN THE MUSEO Correr, on the Grand Canal, there has recently been opened a room containing an assemblage of life-sized mannikins dressed in the various costumes of the *sette cento.*

Here are the red-robed Senator, the proud Procuratessa in brocade and Murano lace, the Abatino in

---

Edith Wharton was born into New York high society, but she threw it all away in 1907 and boated off to Europe with Henry James. There she wrote her best books: New England tragedies, including Ethan Frome, *and satires of New York society, such as* The Age of Innocence.

his plum coloured taffeta coat and black small-clothes, the fashionable reveller in *bauto* and mask, the lacquey in livery of pale-blue silk, the lawyer, the gondolier, the groom, and the noble Marquess in his hunting-dress of white buckskin. Surely nowhere else does one come into such actual contact with that little world which was so essentially a world of *appearances*—of fine clothes, gay colours and graceful courtly attitudes. The mannikins indeed are not graceful. The Cavaliere Leandro can no longer execute a sweeping bow at the approach of the Procuratessa, or slip a love-letter into the muff of the charming Angelica; the Senator may stare as haughtily as he pleases at the Abate and the lawyer, without compelling those humble clients to stir an inch from his path; and the noble Marquess, in his spotless buckskin leggings and gauntlets, will never again be off to shoot thrushes from a "bird-tower" in the Euganeans. But the very rigidity of their once supple joints seems an allegory of their latter state. There they stand, poor dolls of destiny, discarded playthings of the gods, in attitudes of puzzled wonder, as if arrested in their revels by the stroke of the dread Corsican magician—for it was not Death but Napoleon who "stepped tacitly and took them" from the plots and pleasures, the sunshine and music of the canals, to that pale world of oblivion where only now and then some dreamer curious of the day of little things revisits their melancholy ghosts.

Permission acknowledgments

Excerpt from *Death in Venice* by Thomas Mann ©1963 by Alfred A.
Knopf. Reprinted by permission of Vintage Books, a division of Random
House, Inc.

Excerpt from "The Queen of Spades" from *The Passion* by Jeanette Winterson
©1987 by Jeanette Winterson. Reprinted by permission of Vintage Books,
a division of Random House, Inc.

Excerpt from *My Venetian Window* by Jean Paul Sartre from *Venice Desired* by
Tony Tanner, translated by Tony Tanner ©1992 by Tony Tanner.
Reprinted by permission of Harvard University Press.

"The Venetian Mask" from *The Last Italian* by William Murray ©1991 by
William Murray. Reprinted by permission of Touchstone Books, a division
of Simon & Schuster, Inc.

"Churchill in Venice" by Orson Welles from *This Is Orson Welles* by Orson
Welles and Peter Bogdanovich, edited by Jonathan Rosenbaum ©1992 by
Oja Kodar, Jonathan Rosenbaum, and Peter Bogdanovich. Reprinted by
permission of HarperCollins Publishers.

"Venice Letter" by Ezra Pound from *Ezra Pound and Dorothy Shakespeare:
Their Letters 1909-1914* edited by Omar Pound and A. Walton Litz ©1984
by Michael B. Yeats. Reprinted by permission of New Directions.

THE WISDOM OF THE GREEK FATHERS

THE WISDOM
OF THE
GREEK FATHERS

Compiled by Andrew Louth

This edition copyright © 1997
Lion Publishing

Published by
Lion Publishing plc
Sandy Lane West, Oxford, England
ISBN 0 7459 3727 6

First edition 1997
10 9 8 7 6 5 4 3 2 1 0

A catalogue record for this book is
available from the British Library

Printed and bound in Singapore

Series editor: Philip Law

Project editor: Angela Handley

Book designer: Nicholas Rous

Jacket designer: Gerald Rogers

CONTENTS

INTRODUCTION

Central to the vision of the Greek Fathers is their sense of the paradox of God's distance and his closeness, his majesty and his nearness. On the one hand, God is utterly beyond anything we can know or imagine: he is transcendently unknowable – they would have applauded the opinion of the pagan Greek philosopher, Damascius, who said, 'we do not even know whether he is unknowable.' On the other hand, God, as the source of all being, as the source of our being, is closer to us than we are to ourselves.

But for the Greek Fathers this is more than just an intellectual paradox about transcendence and immanence. For in Christ the transcendent God has become a human being just like us: the intellectual paradoxes of the infinitely distant and infinitely close are *historically* true of the one the gospels call Jesus of Nazareth, the one born in a stable, the one who died on the cross. The paradoxes intensify as the source of life comes into being in the womb of Mary, the

'Bearer of God', and life succumbs to death on the cross, only to be manifest as life triumphant over death in the resurrection. 'Christ has risen from the dead, by death he has trampled on death, and to those in the tombs given life!' – as Greek Christians, Orthodox Christians, sing, with inexhaustible joy, as they celebrate the resurrection at Easter.

But the paradoxes do not end there either. For the Greek Fathers 'theology' is not an intellectual exercise, whether practised on matters philosophical or historical: it is an experience, realized in prayer, made possible through responding to God's self-emptying love in the incarnation by our own attempts at ascetic struggle and self-denying love. This experience is transforming, transfiguring: its 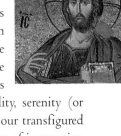 fruits are the virtues of faith, humility, serenity (or 'dispassion'), but what we become in our transfigured state is God himself. So to the paradox of incarnation – God become a man – there corresponds the paradox of deification – the human person transfigured by, and into, God. And all this is celebrated in the services of the church, the liturgy, preeminently the Eucharistic

Liturgy, in which the whole material creation — bread and wine, water and oil, smells and colours, music and shape, the beauty of creation and the art of human creativity — is drawn into the celebration of God's transfiguring love for the whole of his creation.

The passages that follow are taken from a few of the Fathers from the period after the conversion of the Emperor Constantine (in 312), the period during which Christian ideals were gradually inculcated into the Roman empire. Looking back, Christians have mixed feelings about the union of political power and the Christian gospel. But what was realized in that period was an understanding of a Christianity that saw no limits to the transforming power of divine grace. The loving power of the All-ruling One, the *Pantocrator*, whose gaze looked down from the dome of the church, was not limited to the community gathered beneath, it was not even limited to the supposedly universal sovereignty of the emperor: it was infinite and embraced the whole of the created cosmos. It is that vision that this little book may help us to glimpse.

ANDREW LOUTH

GOD

DEITY

God is one, unoriginate, incomprehensible, possessing completely the total potentiality of being, altogether excluding notions of when and how, inaccessible to all, and not to be known through any natural image by any creature.

Maximus the Confessor (580–662)

WONDER OF GOD

There are many things I simply wonder at, but without fear, such as the beauty of columns, a fresco, a body in the flower of youth. Again we wonder at the extent and unfathomable depth of the sea, but with fear, when we lean over its depths. It is like this when the prophet leans over the immense and unbounded lake of God's wisdom, and goes dizzy, amazed, he recoils with a great fear, and cries out, saying, 'I will confess to you that you have amazed me fearfully; your works are marvellous.' And again, 'Your knowledge of me has amazed me: it is too strong for me, I cannot attain it' (Psalms 138:6).

John Chrysostom (c. 349–407)

BOUNDLESSNESS OF GOD

No matter how long you might stay at the spring, you would always be beginning to see the water. For the water never stops flowing, and it is always beginning to bubble up again. It is the same with one who fixes his gaze on the infinite beauty of God. It is constantly being discovered anew, and it is always seen as something new and strange in comparison with what the mind has always understood. And as God continues to reveal himself, man continues to wonder…

Gregory of Nyssa (c. 337–95)

GOD AS SPIRIT

But the Lord calls it the 'voice of a gentle breeze' (1 Kings 19:12 LXX). For God is breath, and the breath of the wind is shared by all; nothing shuts it in, nothing holds it prisoner.

Maximus the Confessor

CREATION OUT OF LOVE

We must dare to add this as being no less true:
that the Source of all things Himself, in His
wonderful and good love for all this, through
the excess of His loving goodness, is carried
outside Himself, in His providential care for
all that is, so enchanted is He in goodness and
love and longing. Removed from His position
above all and beyond all, He descends to be in
all according to an ecstatic and transcendent
power which is yet inseparable from Himself.

Dionysius the Areopagite (?early sixth century)

CREATION

REVEALING GOD

If sometime, then, in a serene night, you gaze
up at the ineffable beauty of the stars, you can
form an idea of the creator of the universe,
who has embroidered the sky with these
flowers, and how in what you see necessity
takes the form of the delightful; again, during
the day, if you consider the wonders of the day
with sober thought, and from what you see
form an idea of what is invisible, you will
become a hearer, fit and made ready for the
fullness of this solemn and blessed theatre.

Basil the Great (c. 330–79)

MATTER

I do not venerate matter, but the Creator of matter, who became matter for my sake, and accepted to dwell in matter, and through matter worked my salvation; therefore I will not cease to reverence matter, through which my salvation was worked.

John Damascene (c. 675–750)

HUMAN CREATION

For they say that God and the human person
are paradigms one of another, that as much as
God is humanized through love for humankind, so much is the human person able to be
deified through love.

For humanity clearly has the power
of naturally uniting [the divisions of the
cosmos]; through that capacity it can come
to be the way of fulfilment of what is divided
and be openly instituted in itself as the great
mystery of the divine purpose… For this reason
the human person was introduced last among
beings, as a kind of natural bond mediating
between the extremities, and leading into
union in itself those things that are naturally
set apart from one another by a great interval.

Maximus the Confessor

SIN AND THE FALL

THE FALL

The very act of sacred knowledge teaches us that that natural sense of the soul is single, but that it has been divided into two by Adam's disobedience. It will become single and simple again when the Holy Spirit comes into it, something that can only be known by those who have willingly detached themselves from the fair things of this life through hope of good things to come, and drained all the longing of the bodily senses through self-control.

Diadochus of Photike (mid-fifth century)

MARRING THE DIVINE IMAGE

The whole procession of sin entered into human life for its undoing, and from a tiny source poured out upon humankind an infinite sea of evil. The soul's divine beauty, that had been an imitation of its archetype [i.e., God: cf. Genesis 1:26], was, like a blade, darkened with the rust of sin; it no longer kept the beauty of the image it once possessed by nature, and was transformed into the ugliness of sin.

Gregory of Nyssa

REDEMPTION

You brought us out of non-existence into
being, and when we had fallen you raised us
up again, and left nothing undone until you
had brought us up to heaven and had granted
us your Kingdom that is to come. For all
these things we give thanks to you, and to
your only-begotten Son and your Holy Spirit;
for all benefits that we have received, known
and unknown, manifest and hidden.

Liturgy of St John Chrysostom

INCARNATION

A NEW THING

Being perfect God, he became perfect man, and
accomplished the newest of all new things, the only
new thing under the sun (cf. Ecclesiastes 1:9f.).

John Damascene

ADORATION OF THE CHILD

Today the Virgin gives birth to him
    who is above all being,
and the earth offers a cave to him
    whom no one can approach.

Angels with shepherds give glory,
    and Magi journey with a star,
for to us there has been born
    a little Child, God before the ages.

Romanus the Singer (mid-sixth century)

DEIFICATION

For the Word of God became a human being
that we might become God; and he manifested
himself in a body, that we might gain an idea
of the invisible Father; and he endured
insolence from men, that we might inherit
immortality.

Athanasius (c. 290–373)

THE VIRTUES

LOVE

Love is a holy state of the soul, disposing it to value knowledge of God above all created things. We cannot attain lasting possession of such love while we are still attached to anything worldly.

Maximus the Confessor

Love, by its nature, is a resemblance to God, insofar as this is humanly possible. In its activity it is inebriation of the soul. Its distinctive character is to be a fountain of faith, an abyss of patience, a sea of humility.

John Climacus (?seventh century)

FAITH

The deep waters of faith seem turbulent
when we peer into them too curiously; but
when contemplated in a spirit of simplicity,
they are calm. The depths of faith are like the
waters of Lethe, making us forget all evil; they
will not reveal themselves to the scrutiny of
meddlesome reasoning. Let us therefore sail
these waters with simplicity of mind, and so
reach the harbour of God's will.

Diadochus of Photike

HUMILITY

Repentance lifts one up. Mourning knocks at heaven's gate. Holy humility opens it. This I say, and I worship a Trinity in Unity and a Unity in Trinity. The sun lights up everything visible. Humility reaches across everything done according to reason. Where there is no light, all is in darkness. Where there is no humility, all is rotten.

John Climacus

DISPASSION

Stars adorn the skies and dispassion has
the virtues to make it beautiful. By dispassion
I mean a heaven of the mind within the heart...
One is truly dispassionate... when one has
lifted one's mind above everything created,
and has made it master of all the senses;
when one keeps one's soul continually in the
presence of the Lord and reaches out beyond
the borderline of strength to Him.

John Climacus

ADVANCE IN VIRTUE

But here we have a very great paradox:
motion and stability are the same. For usually
speaking, one who is rising is not standing
still, and one who is standing still is not
rising. But here one arises precisely because
one is stationary. This means that one
advances further on the path of perfection
precisely insofar as one remains fixed and
immovable in good… One's very stability
becomes as a wing in one's flight towards
heaven; and the heart becomes winged
because of one's stability in good.

Gregory of Nyssa

PRAYER AND
THE KNOWLEDGE
OF GOD

THEOLOGY

If you are a theologian, you pray truly;
if you pray truly, you are a theologian.

Evagrius (346–99)

PRAYER FOR DAILY BREAD

May you give bread; that is to say, let us have nourishment from our just efforts. If your profit does not belong to others, if your income is not the result of another's tears, if no one is hungry because you are full, if no one groans because of your abundance, such then is the bread of God, the fruit of justice, the ear of the corn of peace, undefiled by being mixed with the seed of tares. But if you cultivate what belongs to others and fill your eyes with injustice, confirming your unjust gains with written documents, then you may indeed say to God: 'Give bread', but another will hear this cry of yours, not God. One who pursues righteousness receives bread from God, whereas the man who cultivates injustice is fed by the inventor of injustice.

Gregory of Nyssa

PRAYER IN TRANQUILLITY

We must try to keep the mind in tranquillity. For just as the eye which is constantly moving about, now turning from side to side, now incessantly peering up and down, cannot see clearly what lies before it, but the sight must be fixed firmly on the object in view if its vision is to be clear, so too the human mind when distracted by countless worldly cares cannot reach out clearly to the truth… From all this there is but one escape – separation from the world altogether. But withdrawal from the world does not mean being outside it bodily, but breaking off the soul from sympathy with the body…; it also means being ready to receive in one's heart the impressions engendered there by divine instruction…

What then is more blessed than to imitate on earth the chorus of the angels; to hasten to prayer at the very break of day, and to worship our Creator with hymns and songs; then, when the sun shines brightly and we turn to our tasks, prayer attending us wherever we go, to season our labours with sacred song as food with salt? For that state of the soul in which there is joy and no sorrow is a blessing bestowed by the consolation of hymns.

Basil the Great

PRAYER AND UNKNOWING

One who stands beside the sea sees the
infinite ocean of the waters, but cannot grasp
the extent of them, beholding only a part.
So it is with one who is judged worthy to
fix his gaze in contemplation on the infinite
ocean of God's glory and behold him with the
intelligence: he sees not how great God is, but
only what the spiritual eyes of his soul can
grasp… Just as one who enters the waters of
the sea up to his knees or his waist sees clearly
what is outside the water, but if he plunges
into the depths and is wholly covered by water,
can no longer see anything outside the water,
and knows nothing else than that he is in the
depths of the sea, so it is with those who
increase in spiritual progress and come to the
perfection of knowledge and contemplation.

Symeon the New Theologian (949–1022)

UNITED WITH THE DAZZLING RAYS

And this is, moreover, the most divine knowledge of God, that He is known through unknowing, according to the union which transcends the understanding, when the understanding withdraws from all, and abandons itself, and is united with the dazzling rays and in them and from them is enlightened by the unsearchable depths of wisdom.

Dionysius the Areopagite

PRAYER AS GRACE

So let us stretch ourselves in prayers upward to the more lofty elevation of the kindly Rays of God. Imagine a great shining chain hanging downward from the heights of heaven to the world below. We grab hold of it with one hand and then another, and we seem to be pulling it down towards us. Actually it is already there on the heights and down below and instead of pulling it to us we are being lifted upwards to that brilliance above, to the dazzling light of those beams.

Dionysius the Areopagite

PRAYER AS CUTTING AWAY

For this is to see and to know truly, and to praise in a transcendent way Him who is beyond being through the negation of all things, just as those who make statues with their own hands cut away everything which obscures the clear beholding of the hidden form, and thus make it manifest its hidden beauty solely by the process of cutting away.

Dionysius the Areopagite

PRAYER OF QUESTIONING TRUST

And where now? Tell me, God the Word.
To that unshakeable dwelling-place,
   I beseech you,
To my Trinity that shines forth
   an undivided radiance,
In whose beams let me be gently lifted up.

Gregory Nazianzen (329–89)

THE CHURCH

An Earthly Heaven

The church is the temple of God, a sacred precinct, a house of prayer, the assembly of the people, the body of Christ. Its name is the bride of Christ. It has been cleansed by the water of His baptism, sprinkled by His blood and adorned in bridal array, and sealed with the ointment of the Holy Spirit… The church is an earthly heaven, in which the God beyond the heavens dwells and walks about.

It represents the crucifixion, burial and resurrection of Christ: it is glorified more than Moses' tabernacle of witness, in which were the mercy seat and the Holy of Holies. It is prefigured in the patriarchs, foretold in the prophets, founded in the apostles, adorned by hierarchs and fulfilled in martyrs.

Germanus of Constantinople (c. 634–733)

SYMBOLS OF THE FUTURE

We are ordered to perform in this world the symbols and signs of the future things so that, through the service of the Sacrament, we may be like men who enjoy symbolically the happiness of the heavenly benefits, and thus acquire a sense of possession and a strong hope of the things for which we look.

Theodore of Mopsuestia (c. 350–428)

THE FINAL WORD

Glory to God for everything!

*John Chrysostom's last words, as he died in exile
(also his habitual exclamation)*

Text Acknowledgments

Extracts 1 (*Centuries on Theology* I.1.) and 16 (*Century on Spiritual Knowledge* 22) are taken from *The Philokalia: The Complete Text*, ed. and trans. by G.E.H. Palmer, Philip Sherrard and Kallistos Ware, Vol. 2, Faber and Faber, 1981, pages 114, 258. Extract 2: *On the Incomprehensibility of God* I.202–12. Extracts 3 (*Homilies on the Song of Songs* 11), 10 (*On Virginity* 12 (Gregorii Nysseni Opera 8.1) and 19 (*Life of Moses* II.243–44) are taken from *From Glory to Glory*, selected and introduced by Jean Danielou, trans. and ed. by Herbert Musurillo, John Murray, 1962, pages 246, 113, 149–50. Extract 4: *Scholia on the Divine Names* I.4 (208.3). Extract 5: *Divine Names* 4. 13 (ed. Suchla, 159). Extract 6: *Hexaemeron* 6. 1 (117BC). Extract 7: *On the Divine Images*. I.16 (Kotter, vol. 3, p. 89). Extract 8: *Ambigua* 10.3 (1113B) and 41 (1305BC). Extract 9: *Chapters on Spiritual Knowledge* 25. Extract 11 is taken from *The Divine Liturgy of our Father among the Saints, John Chrysostom, the Greek text…*, Oxford University Press, 1995, page 31. Extract 12: *On the Orthodox Faith* 45 (Kotter, vol. 2, p. 108). Extract 13 (*Kontakion on the Nativity* prelude) is taken from *Kontakia On the Life of Christ: Romanus the Melodist*, trans. by Archimandrite Ephrem Lash, HarperCollins, 1996, page 3. Extract 14: *On the Incarnation* 54. Extract 15 (*Ladder of Divine Ascent* 30) is from *The Philokalia: The Complete Text*, ed. and trans. by G.E.H. Palmer, Philip Sherrard and Kallistos Ware, Vol. 1, Faber and Faber, 1979, page 258. Extracts 15 (*Centuries on Love* I.1.), 17 (*Ladder of Divine Ascent* 25) and 18 (*Ladder of Divine Ascent* 29) are taken from *John Climacus: Ladder of Divine Ascent*, trans. by Colm Luibheid and Norman Russell, Paulist Press, 1982, pages 286, 221 and 282. Extract 20: *On Prayer* 61. Extract 21: *On the Lord's Prayer* 4 (Gregorii Nysseni Opera 7.2, ed. Callahan, p. 55, l. 20 p. 56, l. 12). Extract 22 (to his friend, *Ep.* 2 (his friend St Gregory Nazianzen). Extract 23: *Theological Centuries* II.11, 14. Extract 24: *Divine Names* 7.3 (ed. Suchla, 198). Extract 25 (*Divine Names* 3.1) is taken from *Pseudo-Dionysius: The Complete Works*, trans. by Colm Luibheid and Paul Rorem, Paulist Press, 1987, page 68. Extract 26: *Mystical Theology* 2 (ed. Ritter, 145). Extract 27: *Poem on his own life* 1944–48. Extract 28: *On the Divine Liturgy* 1 (ed. Meyendorff, 56). Extract 29 (*Homilies on the Eucharist and the Liturgy* 5) is taken from *Woodbrooke Studies*, Vol. 6, ed. and trans. by A. Mingana, W. Heffer and Sons Ltd, Cambridge, 1933, page 82.

Picture Acknowledgments

Page 1 (Virgin and child, Kykko Monastery, Cyprus); pages 2 and 3 (mosaics from the monastery of Hosios Lukas, 11th century; from left to right: St Thomas, St Matthew, St Philip, St John); page 7 and 47 (mosaic of Christ, Kariye Camii, Istanbul, 14th century); page 9 (The Ascension), page 15 (the Eucharist), page 19 (The Crucifixion), page 23 (The Nativity), page 27 (Christ washing the disciples' feet), page 33 (The Transfiguration), page 43 (The Pentecost) – all from Church of the Holy Cross, Platanistasa, Cyprus, 15th century; pages 10, 13, 24, 34, 41 and 44 (apostle from the monastery of St John Lampadistis, Kalopanayiotis, Cyprus); pages 17 and 29 (ceiling boss from the monastery of St John Lampadistis, Kalopanayiotis, Cyprus) – all courtesy of Sonia Halliday photographs.

Page 4 (mosaics in Dome, Kariye Camii, Istanbul; page 30 (Apostles, 20th century icon); page 37 (Isaiah, 20th century icon); page 39 (David, 20th century icon) – all courtesy of Jonathan Williams.